MURDER AND A CHRISTMAS GIFT

A 1920S HISTORICAL COZY MYSTERY: AN EVIE PARKER MYSTERY BOOK 7

SONIA PARIN

ISBN 9798640773804

CHAPTER 1

Not a creature was stirring, not even a mouse...

Early December, 1920
Halton House, Berkshire

*E*vie scurried across the main hall and burst into the dining room, eager for a cup of hot coffee. All the fires in the house had been lit but she could still feel a light chill in the air.

"Good morning, Ed....*gar.*" Stopping at the door to the breakfast room she sent her gaze skating from one end to the other. "Edgar?" She took a tentative step inside. When she called out again, her voice hitched up, "*Edgar.*"

No sign of her butler or even a footman.

Retracing her steps, she found herself standing in the middle of the hall and looking up at the Woodridge ancestors who gazed down at her, their noble expressions indifferent to her puzzlement. All except for the second Earl, who smiled down at her. Although the mischievous twinkle in his eyes suggested that he too was impervious to her plea.

"Where is everyone?" her voice echoed but no one replied. "It's not my birthday," Evie whispered. Besides, no one would really think of hiding in order to then surprise her. Certainly not so early in the morning.

Squaring her shoulders, she walked into the library. The room felt toasty and welcoming. Yet, she found it empty. Continuing on to the drawing room, she expected to find someone working on their morning correspondence. The previous week, the dowagers had moved into Halton House; a temporary measure when a deluge had revealed the dower house roof to be in desperate need of repair.

Evie saw Sara's embroidery basket but no sign of her mother-in-law. As she turned, she caught sight of Henrietta's spectacles sitting on a desk beside a letter, which meant the post had arrived and there had been someone to receive and distribute the letters.

Something had prompted the dowager to abandon her correspondence and...

Clearly, at one point, there had been people about.

So... Where were they now?

She made her way to the main stairs and continued on along a side hallway where she found the door leading down to the kitchens. "I'm bound to find someone there, surely. And why am I talking to myself?"

Evie flew down the flight of stairs and, reaching the kitchen, she came to an abrupt stop. Empty.

With her heart thumping all the way to her throat, Evie pressed her hand against her chest, and rushed out the back door leading to the cobblestone yard.

The estate workers began their day early, even in winter time. When she reached the middle of the yard, she slowed down, and despite knowing she wouldn't get an answer, she called out, "Hello?"

Reason told her she had no need to panic. If something had happened, someone would have alerted her. In fact, she would have been the first person to be informed.

Calming her breath, Evie folded her arms against the morning chill and strained to hear something, anything.

She walked along the path that led to the garage and the stables, scanning her surroundings for signs of activity; still hopeful of finding someone.

Had she forgotten she needed to be somewhere?

Again, impossible. If that had been the case, someone would have alerted her.

Then she heard it.

A gasp.

A collective gasp.

She looked toward the stables.

Had everyone at Halton House been herded into the stables? What if they were being held captive and at gunpoint?

The next sound she heard sounded like a chorus of exclamations.

Evie looked over her shoulder. Instinct told her to run back to the house, collect Seth, who was no doubt still in bed, and contact the local constabulary.

The seven-year-old Earl of Woodridge had arrived a couple of days before to spend the Christmas holiday with them. In case of any emergency, his safety would be of paramount importance. What if she was too late? What if Seth had been wrenched from his bed and dragged to the stables?

Nonsense. She would have been taken too.

Regardless, she turned to rush back inside. However, she then heard a rapturous round of applause.

More intrigued than fearful now, she turned back toward the stables and took a few determined steps. Coming up to a window, she peered inside.

"Heavens!"

Evie eased the door open far enough to slip inside the stables. She must have stood there for a good five minutes before anyone noticed her.

Everyone from Edgar, the butler, to Lillie, the maid who lit her fire in the morning, stood by watching Seth sitting on a pony, trotting from one end of the stables to the other with Tom Winchester running alongside him on one side and Caro, her maid, on the opposite side, their hands ready to catch the seven-year-old Earl of Woodridge in case he happened to slip off his saddle.

Encouragement followed him every step of the way with her granny, Toodles, cheering the loudest.

For a split second, Evie felt surprised to see her. After delaying her return to America, her granny had then decided she had no desire to risk an encounter with an iceberg and would spend Christmas as Halton House.

The dowagers, Henrietta and Sara, stood beside her urging the young Lord Woodridge to break into a canter.

Everyone remained oblivious of Evie standing by the door and she almost felt compelled to sneak out and let them continue enjoying themselves but that would have meant missing out on the sight of young Seth's enjoyment.

His eyebrows were knitted together in deep

concentration while his lips were stretched as wide as they could go into a bright smile.

Only two years before he had lost both parents within a short time. His father had perished in the trenches while his mother had succumbed to the Spanish flu. If he still felt the pain of his loss, he did not show it.

For most people, life went on and everyone found a way to keep going, learning to carry the extra burden of their experiences.

Both pony and rider trotted toward Evie's end of the stables, Seth's two abled assistants still running alongside him.

Then one of the maids shifted and in doing so, she caught sight of Evie. Bobbing a curtsey, she nudged the maid beside her who then also bobbed a curtsey. They both rushed out of the stable but not before alerting the people near them.

One by one, the spectators became aware of Evie and left in a hurry as if suddenly remembering they had pressing matters to attend to.

Edgar must have been held enthralled by Seth's horse-riding. Only when the stables emptied of all the house staff did he finally notice everyone's absence. Looking around him, he then saw Evie.

Edgar's cheeks colored. Giving his sleeves a firm tug, he straightened and walked toward her, inclining his head slightly as he said, "My lady. Good morning."

"Edgar. If I'd known everyone would be down here, I would have made a point of coming down earlier. When did this happen? How? And where did that pony come from?"

Edgar cleared his throat. "Well… I'm not sure, my lady." He looked about him. "If you'll excuse me I… I have matters to attend to."

Henrietta clapped her hands. "Evangeline. You've been missing out on all the fun."

"Yes, I can see that. Why didn't anyone tell me?"

"Good morning, Birdie."

"Good morning, Granny."

"It all happened so quickly," Toodles said. "One moment we were settling down to breakfast and the next, here we were."

Henrietta nodded. "Yes. I had been attending to my correspondence. It all happened very quickly…"

"And no one thought to tell me?" Evie murmured.

"Everyone assumed you'd be asleep," Henrietta said.

"That's what happens when you play lady of the manor and sleep in, Birdie."

"I do not… Oh, never mind." Looking around the near empty stables, she added, "I feel like a Scrooge, ruining everyone's fun."

Finally, Tom looked up. Smiling, he took hold of the reins and slowed the pony down.

Evie smiled. "Good morning, Seth."

"Cousin Evie. Did you see me ride?" Seth asked.

Happy he had finally become accustomed to calling her Cousin Evie instead of Lady Woodridge, she nodded. "I did. You looked splendid."

"Everyone said you wouldn't mind."

Seeing his worried expression, Evie wondered how she had been looking at him. "Of course, I don't mind." Only… she did.

As Nicholas' heir, Seth had a huge amount of responsibility to face when he grew up and Evie felt responsible for ensuring he actually grew up.

Tom helped him dismount and handed the reins to a stable hand. "Countess, you missed out on a lot of fun."

"So everyone keeps telling me."

"Milady." Caro grinned. "Come along, milord. Breakfast awaits you." Before Evie could say anything, Caro hurried out of the stables with Seth in tow.

"Birdie. Why are you frowning? Anyone would think you disapprove," her granny said.

Evie clasped and wrung her hands together. "I came down for breakfast and found the place empty."

"She's feeling left out," Henrietta murmured.

"I would too, in her place," Sara declared. "I told Henrietta someone needed to fetch you."

"Yes, and I remember saying Evangeline is a Countess and therefore, she is not to be *fetched* as if she were a basket." Henrietta smiled at Evie. "Somewhere in the midst of the squabble, we forgot about you. Well, fun's over and I am famished. Shall we go in to breakfast?"

The dowagers and Toodles made their way back to the house leaving Evie still frowning and looking straight at Tom.

"Did you organize this?" she asked.

"The pony? Yes."

"When?"

He looked up in thought. "A couple of days ago. I happened to be down in the village. Remember, I told you I'd heard about a new man who has experience with roadsters. Anyhow, I bumped into Charlie Timms and asked if he had any ponies."

Charlie Timms... The local breeder. Evie looked around the stables as if searching for something when in fact, she was trying to settle her thoughts. "I guess I must have missed hearing about your plans to get Seth a pony."

"He asked for one."

"Pardon? When?"

"I'm not sure."

"Did he ask you directly?"

"Come along, Countess. Breakfast will get cold."

"Are you trying to avoid answering me?"

"That depends. Are you going to accuse us of pandering to Seth's every whim and spoiling him?"

"Well… Is that what you are doing? Hang on… Us? Who else is in on it?"

"I think I've said too much," Tom murmured under his breath.

Evie accepted another cup of coffee from Edgar. As she drank it, she studied the dowagers sitting across the table. Since settling down to breakfast, no one had mentioned the early morning excitement. Instead, Henrietta had been talking about the letter she had received from an old friend.

"She stayed with us for two months while her parents traveled in Europe. We were both sixteen and in love with the same young man who happened to be quite unsuitable."

"Let me guess," Toodles said, "he didn't have a title."

"On the contrary. As the first born, he stood to inherit his father's dukedom. Just think of it, I would have been a duchess."

Intrigued, Toodles leaned forward and lowered her voice to a whisper. "What happened?"

"My father forbade any association with him because he had a reputation for being a philanderer. He had a love of horses and gambling and nothing else."

"If everyone knew him to be a philanderer, he must have loved women," Toodles reasoned.

"Yes, I suppose so... But one didn't talk about that. Anyhow, she writes to tell me her daughter-in-law, the current duchess, has produced nothing but girls and now the estate must go to a distant cousin several times removed. Or at least, what's left of the estate. Getting all those daughters settled is a drain on any family. In this day and age, we witness so many changes... almost daily, but the burden of marriage settlements remain an unchanging constant. I believe they are currently looking for a wealthy American."

Evie glanced away from Henrietta in time to catch Toodles looking at Tom. She'd almost believe her grandmother thought Tom might fit the bill, but that could only be possible if he had spun her the tale about striking it rich in the Oklahoma oilfields...

"There are plenty of American millionaires floating around the place, Henrietta," Toodles said.

"Yes, that's what I intended saying to her, but there is no point in offering encouragement without also including some useful information."

"Such as?" Toodles asked.

"Specifics, my dear Toodles. Where exactly can one find one of these rich Americans?"

"They could try Cowes," Sara remarked.

"What and where is that?" Toodles asked.

"It's in the Isle of Wight. The cream of English society spends a week there enjoying the full social life of Cowes Week. The Duke of Malborough's brother found himself an American bride there."

Henrietta exclaimed, "Heavens, Sara. That was so long ago, I can't even remember… oh, yes. In the 1850s. My mother's time!"

"Then it should be easier now," Sara reasoned.

"Easier?" Henrietta asked. "How so?"

"Oh… I don't know. I suppose there must be more Americans visiting now."

"Maybe your friend should pack her granddaughter off to America. That way, she gets the pick of the crop before they sail here," Toodles suggested. "I'll be happy to introduce her around."

Henrietta took a sip of her tea. "I hope you realize, there is no title to be gained, only the prestige of being married to a lady."

"Well, that's something."

As the dowagers and Toodles ironed out the details of a plan they might or might not put into action, Evie turned to Tom. Feeling no qualms about addressing the subject Tom seemed intent on avoiding, she asked, "What else has Seth asked for?"

He looked up from his bacon and eggs. "Pardon?"

"Seth. You said he asked for a pony. I want to know if he has asked for anything else."

"Oh." Tom drained his cup of coffee and sat back. Edgar approached and offered more. "Thank you,

Edgar. You are always several steps ahead, anticipating everyone's needs."

"I can only try to do my best, Mr. Winchester."

As Tom returned his attention to Evie, Henrietta mused, "I've heard say there is a disturbing shortage of eligible men. Some believe there will be an entire generation of women who will remain spinsters."

"Heavens," Sara exclaimed.

"It's the lost generation, you see," Henrietta continued. "All those men who perished in the Great War…"

Unbelievable, Evie thought. If she didn't know better, she'd think everyone wished to change the subject.

"And what are you getting up to today, Birdie?" her granny asked.

"Tom and I are going into the village." That would give her the perfect opportunity to question him without interruptions. "One of the villagers has been ill and we're taking a basket." She looked at Tom as if daring him to back out of the outing.

Tom smiled at Toodles. "Well, that's me taken care of. What are you ladies getting up to today?"

Toodles shrugged. "Oh… nothing much…"

Henrietta nodded. "I suppose I should respond to my friend's letter and tell her there are many prospects in the horizon… or across the ocean."

"I'll be working on my embroidery," Sara said. "Nothing as exciting as going into the village…"

If Evie hadn't been fixated with Tom's evasive actions, she might have sensed a plot in the making. She might even have suspected the dowagers and Toodles of wishing to take advantage of Evie's absence...

CHAPTER 2

All manner of suspicious behavior...

*E*vie reached the gate to the small cottage and turned to wave goodbye to Mrs. Hursley. The visit had served as a distraction, taking her mind off Tom's gift to Seth. She hadn't broached the subject on the drive to the village because Tom had talked incessantly about the new motor car mechanic in the village, but she fully intended asking him about it now.

She slipped on her gloves and walked with determination toward the Duesenberg, reaching it just as Tom came trotting along the street.

"Where did you go?" she asked.

"Here and there," he said and held the passenger door open for Evie.

Noticing the small parcel he held, she asked, "What's that?" When he didn't answer, she waited for him to walk around the motor car and settle in.

"What's in the parcel?" she persevered.

"Oh… I… I picked up a book at the store."

Evie arranged a blanket over her lap and studied the package. "What sort of book?"

"It's an adventure story. Nothing you'd be interested in."

"Nice wrapping," she said. "The store went to a lot of trouble for you."

Tom waited for a motor car to drive by and then got them on their way. "Oh, yes. Very attentive. How is Mrs. Hursley?"

"Who?"

"The woman you visited."

"Oh… She's doing splendidly. The neighbor is taking care of her children for a few more days. She's already on her feet and getting up and about… What's it called?"

"Pardon?"

"The book you purchased. What's the title?"

"Book? Oh, this book… It's the Wizard of Oz. I was lucky to find a copy here. I thought I might have to send away for it."

Evie shifted and stared at him, her voice filled with curiosity as she asked, "Is that another gift for Seth?"

Tom shrugged. "Maybe."

Evie took a deep swallow. "But you've given him a pony."

"He can't ride the pony all day long," Tom explained.

"Is it a Christmas gift?"

"I suppose so... What did you get him?"

Evie's voice hitched, "Compared to your pony? What does it matter what I got him? My gift will pale by comparison."

Tom chuckled. "He's a little boy, Countess. I'm sure he'll like anything you give him."

Evie crossed her arms and nibbled the edge of her lip. "It's not easy buying a gift for a boy. I... I got him a jigsaw puzzle... of the world... It's... it's educational. I... I also got him a book. Of course, I can't compete with your pony *or* your book."

"You could give him a model airplane," Tom suggested. "They're all the rage."

Evie lifted her chin.

Clearing his throat, Tom said, "I could tell him the pony is from all of us."

"I wouldn't expect you to do that. What I'd like to know is how on earth you found out what he wanted."

Tom laughed. "All boys want a pony."

"So, he didn't volunteer the information?" She

couldn't remember with any certainty, but she thought Seth had asked for it…

"Would it be a problem if he had?" Tom asked.

Evie studied her gloves and shrugged. "I just don't want him to be spoilt. He already has so much. He needs to learn to appreciate it all." And yet, Evie thought, life had dealt Seth a cruel blow and her instinct urged her to spare him any more cruelty.

"He's only here for the holidays, Countess. Don't you want him to have fun?"

"Of course, I do. But he's not like other children. He's the Earl of Woodridge. He… He has responsibilities. There are many people who will rely on him for their livelihood. Estates such as Halton House don't run themselves…"

"Countess."

Evie took a deep swallow. "Yes?"

"He's seven."

"Yes, but these are his formative years." Evie knew she stood on shaky ground with her argument fast losing credibility.

If she had to be honest, she wished she had thought of getting him a pony instead of a silly jigsaw puzzle. Reason told her he already owned a stable full of horses. But not a pony, a small voice in her head murmured. Well, not until now, the small voice added. "I'm adding salt to my own wound," she whispered.

Oh… Why couldn't she have been the one to give Seth his first pony?

"Yes, he's the Earl of Woodridge," Tom agreed, "but he still needs to learn to ride."

Evie looked out at the gray sky. After a long silence, she said, "Well, I hope you're not feeding him sweets while my back is turned. You'll ruin his teeth."

"I'm sorry. I seem to have overstepped…"

Evie's shoulders dropped. "Oh, for heaven's sake. You didn't."

Tom shook his head. "Next time I plan a surprise, I'll make sure to include you."

Studying her gloves, Evie asked, "Is there anything else I should know about? I can't help feeling there is something going on right under my nose." Evie put her hand up. "Never mind. I just heard myself. Anyone would think I'm suffering from some sort of neurosis."

"Have you been reading Freud again?" Tom asked.

Before she could answer, Tom said, "I know what I'll do. I'll ask Seth what he really wants for Christmas. There's bound to be something really special and then you can get it for him."

Evie wished she'd never brought up the subject. "Let's just forget about it."

"All right then. I won't ask him."

"Oh… Oh, but… I'm sure it wouldn't hurt."

Pulling up her coat collar, Evie hurried inside the house while Tom drove off toward the garage.

"Winter is nipping at our heels, Edgar. The ground feels frozen through and it's not even snowing yet."

"Yes, my lady. It's looking quite cold out there."

Removing her gloves, she made her way toward the stairs only to stop at the sound of laughter. "I seem to be missing out on more fun." Smiling, she swung on her feet and walked toward the drawing room, stopping at the door to finish removing her gloves.

"Six guineas for a week's observation!"

Evie recognized Caro's voice. Not only did her maid sound excited but, judging by the soft thud she heard, Caro was jumping on the spot.

The next voice she heard belonged to Toodles. "Ninety-four pounds for an investigation."

Millicent whooped, "I have a cousin who works in an office and she doesn't get anything near that in an entire year. We'll be swimming in money!"

It didn't surprise Evie to find both her maids in the drawing room but her curiosity had been well and truly piqued. What could they be talking about? And... had they all wanted Evie out of the house so they could talk freely?

Millicent's excitement appeared to be contagious. Evie heard more exclamations and then her granny spoke up again.

"But that's only for one job."

Job? Investigation? What were they talking about?

Walking into the drawing room, Evie took in the happy group. The dowagers were both smiling, Toodles sat by the fireplace, her notebook in hand, while Caro and Millicent stood in front of them, both still jumping on the spot.

"Hello."

Caro swung around. Her cheeks colored as she smiled at Evie. "Milady, we didn't expect you back so soon." She tugged Millicent's hand and pulled her away. "We must be going now. Things to do…Places to be…"

"That's twice in one day," Evie murmured.

"What's that, Birdie?" her granny asked.

Removing her hat and coat, Evie set them down on a chair and walked across the room to sit opposite the dowagers. "My presence seems to be having a curious effect on people today. I either walk into empty rooms or as soon as I appear, people vacate them, beating a hasty retreat."

"How is Mrs. Hursley?" Sara asked.

And then, there was the constant changing of subject, Evie thought…

"I'm happy to report she's already on her feet." Evie turned toward her granny. "So, what were you all talking about?"

Toodles exchanged a look with the dowagers. "Oh… We were… discussing Christmas trees."

Really?

"Yes," Sara said. "We've been… trying to decide the theme for this year."

Evie straightened her skirt. "I thought I heard something about an investigation."

"You must have imagined it, Birdie."

Evie went over what she'd heard. Glancing at her granny, she saw her slip her notebook behind a cushion.

"At last, here's Edgar with afternoon tea." Toodles clapped her hands. "We were beginning to wonder if you'd forgotten us."

"My apologies…"

Edgar looked as though he wished to say more but then the door opened and Caro strode in with Seth.

"Ah, here is Lord Woodridge," Toodles exclaimed. "I see they let you out of the schoolroom."

"Only after a tug-of-war," Caro declared. "The new tutor, Mr. Carsten, is determined Seth will be fluid in French before he leaves here. He doesn't seem to understand he's only seven."

Toodles patted the chair next to her. "You're lucky to have a friend to rescue you from your tutor's clutches."

Seth grinned. "*Oui, Madam.*"

"Surely we could dispense with the lessons until after Christmas." Toodles ruffled his hair. "Soon there'll be snow and you'll want to go out and build a snowman and maybe Tom can find a sled for you."

A sled!

That would be a splendid gift, Evie thought as Edgar handed her a cup of tea.

"I'm sure there's one in the attic somewhere," Henrietta said. "As a young boy, Nicholas used to love sledding down the slopes."

"We'll venture up to the attic tomorrow," Toodles promised, her voice filled with wonderment. "We could have a treasure hunt. I'm sure there are all sorts of interesting things hidden up there."

Henrietta turned to Edgar. "Have the Christmas tree decorations been brought down, Edgar?"

"Not yet, my lady. Perhaps we can do it tomorrow."

"We should go up now," Toodles declared and turned to Seth. "Unless you'd like to stay here and have some cake."

Seth patted his stomach and grinned. "I have already had my fill of cake down in the kitchen."

Caro shook her head as if trying to hush him.

Evie glanced at her maid as she said, "I thought you were in the schoolroom."

"I have been in the kitchen watching Mrs. Horace bake," Seth revealed. "That's when we had hot chocolate and cake."

It seemed Caro had told a little white lie...

"In that case," Toodles said, "we can go up to the attic now."

"But what about your tea?" Evie asked.

"It can wait. There's nothing more thrilling than hunting around for forgotten treasures."

Evie had to agree. Taking a sip of her tea, she smiled. She loved trimming the Christmas tree. The house came alive, more than at any other time during the year. Then, there were the gifts and the singing. The entire week before Christmas remained the busiest time at Halton House. Even during the grim years they'd been able to lift everyone's spirits...

Setting her cup down, she looked up in time to see the back of Henrietta and Sara as they made their way out of the drawing room... hurrying to keep up with Toodles and Seth who had already left.

Evie looked around her.

Everyone had gone to the attic?

And no one had thought to invite her along?

Edgar stood by the tea service looking up at the ceiling.

Once again, she had managed to empty a room without even trying.

Tom walked in and found her gaping.

"What's wrong, Countess?"

Still gaping, Evie told him about everyone going up to the attic in search of the Christmas decorations and a sled.

"That's a fabulous idea," Tom exclaimed.

Before she could respond, Tom hurried out of the drawing room and went in search of the others.

Edgar cleared his throat.

Evie did her best to ignore him but gave up. "Oh, for heaven's sake. I suppose you want to go up too, Edgar. Well… go on. Don't let me stop you."

Her butler did not need to be told twice.

Slumping back in her chair, Evie looked around the empty drawing room. When her gaze landed on the chair where Toodles had been sitting, she remembered her granny's notebook…

Looking over her shoulder toward the door, she made sure she wouldn't be seen prying. "Of course, it would be quite wrong of me to snoop. After all, Granny made a point of putting the notebook under the cushion. However, if she had really wanted to keep it private, she would have taken it with her…"

Surging to her feet, she walked around the drawing room, all the while keeping an eye on the door.

They had been talking about some sort of investigation and Caro and Millicent had both been excited about the sums of money mentioned.

Evie tapped her finger against her chin. A short while ago, her granny and the dowagers had encouraged her to set herself up as a female private investigator.

The idea had seemed ludicrous…

It still did.

Had Toodles decided to go into business for herself?

Weaving her way around a couple of chairs, she eased down on the sofa her granny had occupied.

"Honestly, this is my house. I should feel free to look at anything I find lying around..." Peering down at the cushion, she feigned surprise. "Oh, I wonder what this is? It doesn't look like a private journal." Pulling the notebook by the edge, she eased it away from its hiding place.

"Just one peek inside..."

She was about to turn the page when she heard footsteps approaching. Evie jumped to her feet and hurried to resume her place in the chair opposite.

When Tom entered, he looked around. "Weren't you sitting on the other side?"

"Um... I got up... to stretch my legs." She gave him a wide smile. "Did you find anything up in the attics?"

"I sure did." He took the chair opposite her. "Remember I told you I'd ask Seth what he really wanted for Christmas?"

"Oh, yes..."

"You'll never guess, so I'll tell you." He held up a Christmas decoration.

"What is it? I mean... I know it's a Christmas bauble, but what does it mean? Does he want to put the tree up now? We usually wait until a week before..."

Tom shook his head. "When Edgar pulled out a box of decorations, Seth became pensive. Then he picked up a small carved figure. Caro pressed him for information and he told us he remembered his father had carved a whole set of Christmas decorations for him."

Evie shifted to the edge of the chair. "We put all his family possessions in storage." She shrugged. "What little there was of it. Did Edgar find them?"

"No."

"They must be there."

"Edgar found everything but the decorations."

Evie drummed her fingers on the armrest. "They must be somewhere."

"Henrietta thinks someone might have taken them as a keepsake."

"Does she have anyone in mind?"

Tom brushed his hand across his chin. "Assuming Seth's parents had some servants working for them, they might know something."

Evie sat back and nibbled on the tip of her thumb. "It's just the sort of thing he would remember."

"Yes, and I think it would make him very happy to see them again. He had this look of longing about him. Almost sad."

"He must miss his parents dreadfully," Evie murmured. She'd always been mindful of the painful loss he'd suffered but she had to focus on his future, for his sake. "Christmas is supposed to be a happy time…" Evie shot to her feet. "We must do something about it."

"What do you propose doing?"

"We could drive out to the house where he lived.

The village is not far. Well… it's a couple of hours away, but we shouldn't have any trouble getting there. We could do it in a day. I'm sure the current owners will allow us to look around. They might even know something about the decorations. They're just the sort of thing that can be overlooked and left behind…" She gave a firm nod. "Yes, that's what we'll do. We'll set off early tomorrow morning." Evie smiled. "Oh, Seth will be so happy."

CHAPTER 3

The next day...

The previous day, she had missed her opportunity to see what Toodles had written in her little black book. Now she would have to contrive a way to get her hands on it again...

Evie had spent an entire evening trying to get to the bottom of the conversation she had overheard, and every time she'd tried to bring up the subject, someone had spoken up, triggering a hearty conversation about something else entirely. Even if she had climbed onto a table and performed a dance to get everyone's attention, she believed they would have found a way to change the subject.

When she had retired to her room, Caro had chatted non-stop about Seth and, once again, Evie had failed to discover what they had all been talking about in the drawing room.

"I've packed an extra coat for you, milady. And I labeled the hats and scarves so you'll know which one goes with—"

"Caro, I think I'm quite capable of matching colors."

"Really, milady? Last time you tried it, you came up with orange and green."

"Yes, and what did you do with my dress? You liked it so much, you gave it to a thespian to wear on the stage."

Caro tried to hide her smile as she said, "The thespian needed to be seen from a distance…"

Evie glanced at the suitcase. "We'll only be gone for a day or two. How much have you packed?"

"You never know what you'll need, milady. Best to be prepared, I always say, and with good reason. Did we know it would snow today? No, we didn't." Caro looked up at the clock on the mantle. "You should get going if you want to get there before lunch."

"If I didn't know better I'd say you were trying to get me out of the house."

"The sooner you leave, the sooner you'll return with the decorations. Seth will love you for it. He doesn't even suspect."

Evie tapped her chin. "There was something I

wanted to ask you." Shaking her head, she said, "No, it's gone. I'll probably remember when we're halfway there."

"But you won't turn back. That would be silly. Just write a note to remind yourself to ask me when you return."

"Are you sure you don't want to come with us?" Evie asked and removed a thick woolen scarf she found more practical than stylish. "There's plenty of room in the large motor car."

Caro took the scarf and put it back in the suitcase. Turning, she busied herself tidying up the perfume bottles on the dresser. "Oh, no. I'm sure I'll only be in the way. Besides, Seth is only here for a short while and I want to spend as much time with him as possible."

"Please remember he has his lessons," Evie warned.

Caro huffed. "Why does a seven-year-old boy need to learn Latin? I can understand how French will come in useful. But why Latin? I really don't see the need for it."

"Sometimes I wonder that myself but it's really about learning." Evie nodded. "Yes, he's learning to learn."

Caro snorted. "That's silly. Although... I suppose you're right. As children, we learn nursery rhymes. They don't exactly help us in our adult lives but they were good memory exercises."

"Yes, that's another way of looking at it," Evie

agreed. "Perhaps I should recite a nursery rhyme. It might help me remember what I wanted to ask you... Oh, it's come to me. Yesterday, before I walked into the drawing room, I heard you and Millicent having a conversation with my granny. Toodles mentioned money and an investigation."

"Did she?" Caro could not have sounded more surprised.

"You know very well she did."

Caro handed Evie a pair of gloves only to change her mind and hand her another pair. "You should take this pair as well. It's fur-lined. I'm sure you'll need it on your return. There's no use hoping the weather will improve. At this point, it will only get colder."

"Caro! Please stop avoiding the subject."

Caro looked away. "I suppose I should recite those nursery rhymes too. What did you want to know?"

Evie tapped her foot as she grumbled, "Don't make me repeat myself."

Caro laughed. "You sound just like my mother."

Evie walked to the door and turned the key. When Caro giggled, Evie removed the key and slipped it inside her pocket. "I'm not going anywhere and neither are you until you tell me what you were all talking about."

"I'm not sure what you heard. Your grandmother can be quite amusing. At one point, she had us in stitches."

Employing a no-nonsense tone, Evie demanded, "What is she investigating?"

"Fine, if you must know… Your grandmother telephoned a lady detective."

"What on earth for?"

"She wanted to know if it would be worth your while pursuing a career as a lady detective and…" Caro's eyes sparkled, "it is. She said if you don't take up the profession, she might consider going into it herself and employing us to help her. There's a lot of money to be made and, by the sounds of it, a lot of fun to be had. The lady detective had tons of intriguing tales about her investigations. During a blackmail case, she dressed up as a man and in another investigation, she made herself up to look twenty years older. Can you imagine that? And did I mention the traveling? No, I'm sure I didn't. She goes *everywhere*. Imagine that! Traveling *and* getting paid to do it."

Evie frowned. "So Toodles is *still* trying to lure you away."

Evie settled down in the passenger seat and arranged a blanket over her knees. "Toodles is still trying to steal Caro from me. Can you believe that?" In the same breath, she asked, "Do you know where you're going?" Evie turned around and saw her chauffeur, Edmonds, standing by the porticoed entrance to Halton House shaking his head. "And what is wrong with Edmonds? That's the look of disapproval if ever I saw one and I have seen plenty of them. What does he disapprove of?"

"Which question do you want me to answer first, Countess?" Tom asked as they set off.

"I assume nothing Toodles does surprises you and I'm sure you just spent a considerable amount of time with Edmonds discussing the best routes so you should try to answer the last one."

Tom scratched his head.

"Now I suppose you want me to repeat the question."

"It would help," he murmured as they reached the gatekeeper's cottage.

Mr. Barton stepped out and hurried toward them. "Is that you, milady?"

"Yes, Mr. Barton. You should hurry back inside. It's too cold to be out."

"Are you really headed out in this weather?" Mr. Barton asked.

When Tom didn't answer, Evie smiled. "Needs must, Mr. Barton. We are on a rescue mission."

"Take care and watch those slippery roads, milady."

"Hear that, Tom?"

"Good heavens. Is that another question?" He put the car into gear, drove past the pillared entrance and turned into the road.

Evie shivered. "I hope you've packed a flask. I fear we might need something to warm us up. Did you bring a flask? Yes, I suppose you did. How far is Tring from here?"

"Twenty odd miles."

"Oh, you've found your voice."

"I thought it best to answer quickly before you shot off another fifty questions."

"We'll have to stay alert," Evie said as she fidgeted with her blanket. "I've only been there the one time and there's a tricky turn-off to the house or it's behind a tall hedge. I can't remember which. Of course, there'll be new tenants there now but I'm sure they'll be able to help us." Evie settled back. "I'll try to be an extra set of eyes for you."

"I doubt anyone else is mad enough to be out and about in this weather," Tom remarked.

"You haven't said anything but I suppose you think it's a crazy idea going in search of those decorations. Is that why Edmonds was shaking his head?" Either her chauffeur disapproved of them setting off while it snowed or he was disappointed she hadn't asked him to drive them. "I think we should have asked Edmonds to drive. I fear he might be feeling a little redundant."

Tom glanced at her. Pushing out a breath, he dug inside his coat and retrieved a flask. "And I think you need a shot of this. You sound on edge."

Evie drummed her fingers against her chin. "I

suppose I am a little. What if we don't find the decorations?"

"Then we can say we tried out best, but that's not what you want to hear."

Evie gave it some thought. "You're right. I've adopted entirely the wrong attitude. I should focus on us finding the box of decorations." She gave a firm nod. "Seth is going to be so happy when he sees them. Or will he? Oh, heavens. What if seeing them makes him sad?"

"Countess!" Tom gestured for her to take a drink.

Scooping in a deep breath, she told herself to calm down.

Just as they crossed the village, Evie's gaze landed on the War Memorial. Giving a small shake of her head, she said, "I just want him to be happy and grow up to lead a full life. When did that become a privilege?" She uncapped the flask and took a sip.

"Countess? Wake up."

Startled, Evie yelped. "What's wrong? Why aren't we moving?" She looked ahead and leaned forward to wipe the window. "I can't see anything."

"You've just answered your question."

"Where are we?"

"I'm not sure, but I think we're about three miles from our destination. There's supposed to be a village around here somewhere. We must be close. I'm sure I heard a train whistle."

Evie brushed her hands over her face. "Did I sleep all the way?"

"No, you've only been asleep for about fifteen minutes. This fog came from out of nowhere."

"I'm so sorry, I've been a bad driving companion."

Tom chortled. "I think you exhausted yourself. You've talked non-stop all the way."

"Really? I can't remember what I said."

"You went on about disguising yourself."

"Why would I do that?"

"If you ever become involved in another incident, you thought it would be a good idea. Then you talked at great length about this female detective your grandmother is obsessed with. Anyhow, here we are. We obviously can't stay here. I'm going to get out and try to guide us off the road. There must be a farmhouse around here. You're going to have to drive."

"What?"

"I'll walk a few paces in front to make sure you don't drive into a ditch."

"You can't be serious. In this weather? You'll freeze or disappear into that fog."

"We can't stay here and I can't drive. You should be

able to see me walking ahead. I think it will work. You only need to drive slowly. I'll walk on and try to find a side road. Do you think you can drive slowly?"

Evie lifted her chin. "I can be light on my feet."

Tom laughed. "As opposed to having lead on your feet?"

"I'm sorry to have brought you out here in this weather. And…" Evie wrung her hands together. "I'm glad you got him the pony."

Tom turned his collar up. "What's that got to do with being caught up a fog bank?"

If she hadn't felt the need to match Tom's gift, they would not have driven out…

Evie removed her scarf. "Put this on. It will keep you warm."

Tom looked at the scarf. "Is that green or yellow?"

"Does it matter? I'm sure it will make you more visible. Come on, put it on. Many goats sacrificed their fleece to make it warm."

Tom got out of the motor car and Evie slid over and took her place in the driver's seat.

"I can do this. Yes, I can."

Tom knocked on the window. Winding it down a notch, Evie asked, "Changed your mind?"

"No. Have you?"

"I don't wish to quote the obvious parable about the blind leading the blind…"

Tom nodded. "We'll try to avoid making the situation worse."

Evie watched him walk on ahead. Despite the sound of the motor car, everything around them felt and sounded eerily calm. A thick veil surrounded them. Evie could just make out a few shapes. Mostly trees, she assumed.

"Keep calm. Go slow," she murmured and squinted her eyes. "And, for goodness' sake, do not run Tom over." She could still see his broad shoulders and her scarf. Evie focused on keeping him in sight with such intensity, she nearly missed his hand signal.

"What does that mean? Speed up or slow down?"

Suddenly, he put his hand up, palm facing her.

"Oh, I know that one. Stop."

Tom appeared by the driver's window and knocked on it.

"There's a side road a couple of yards away. I just made out a gate. Let's hope it's open."

Again, he walked ahead and signaled for Evie to turn off the road, which dipped and then rose. After a short distance, Tom came up beside her again.

"The fog appears to be less dense here. I think I can drive the rest of the way."

Evie shifted over to the passenger side. "Thank goodness. My hands are all clammy. But at least I didn't run you over."

"Thank you. I'm rather attached to my life." Tom drove at a cautious pace and managed to stay on the road even as it wound along. "I've never seen such dense fog so far inland."

Just as well they hadn't encountered other motor cars on the road.

He pointed ahead. "And that's fresh snow. I guess winter is really here."

"Oh, there's the house," Evie exclaimed, only now admitting how cold she felt.

As they approached, other vehicles came into view.

"At least we know there's someone home."

Driving past one of the vehicles, Tom turned to look at it. "That one has a flat tire."

Two other motor cars were parked at odd angles. Almost as if the drivers hadn't taken any care.

Tom brought the car to a stop. Before he went around to open her door, a butler appeared.

"My heavens. Do you need assistance?"

Tom walked up to the butler and explained the situation.

The butler nodded. "Welcome to Hills Manor, my lady. This is Sir Kenneth Audrey's house. He will be only too glad to offer you shelter." As he turned to show them through, he stopped and looked into the distance. "Looks like yet another arrival." His eyebrows curved up. "And... It looks rather official... Never mind, do come in."

As Tom cupped her elbow and guided Evie inside, she asked, "Is it my imagination or…

Before she could get the words out, Tom said, "Yes, it's the police."

CHAPTER 4

They stepped inside a spacious hall with a massive stone fireplace at one end.

Evie walked straight toward it. "I didn't want to say anything, but if we had stayed on the road any longer, I might have frozen."

"Yes, your teeth chattered in your sleep." Tom joined her by the fireplace. "Sir Kenneth Audrey? Is he a Knight?"

Evie shrugged. "Or a Baronet."

"How do we find out without asking?"

Evie wiggled her toes and wished she could remove her shoes and stretch her feet out in front of the fire. Settling for holding her hands in front of the delicious warmth, she looked up. "He's a Baronet. See, there's a plaque on that painting with the name."

"So, what do we call him?"

"Let me think…" Evie closed her eyes and tried to remember what she'd been told the first time she'd met a Baronet. "Full name. He'll be announced as Sir Kenneth Audrey. Sir Kenneth Audrey or Sir Kenneth in speech."

Still confused, Tom asked, "Which one?"

"Either one. He'll let you know."

"At least we know he's a welcoming sort." Hearing the front door open again, Tom turned.

The butler stepped aside, allowing two men wearing dark brown coats to enter. Then he showed them through to another room. Closing the door, he turned and approached Evie and Tom. "I will have your luggage brought in momentarily, my lady."

"Oh, I'm sure there's no need for that." Evie looked at Tom. Surely, they would soon be able to set off again.

"It would be quite inadvisable to leave today, my lady. The weather has already worsened and I have just been informed the road conditions have not improved."

"But it would be such an imposition."

"Not at all, my lady. In fact, several others have found themselves in the same predicament. If you'd like, I could show you through to the drawing room now where you will find refreshments. Sir Kenneth will be along shortly." As he turned to lead them through, he added, "By the way, I'm Simmons."

A woman in her sixties with a wild mop of blonde curls showing a hint of gray welcomed them with a wide smile. Evie wished Caro could have been here to see her dress composed of bright yellow sleeves, with the bodice and skirt made up of blocks of purple, green and magenta.

"My lady, this is the Countess of Woodridge and Mr. Tom Winchester."

"Thank you, Simmons." Lady Audrey turned to Evie. "Lady Woodridge. I believe I met your grandmother once."

That did not surprise Evie.

"How is the Dowager Lady Woodridge?"

"She is doing splendidly, Lady Audrey."

"I am so very sorry about this dreadfully unpredictable weather. The road leading here is notorious. Once the fog settles in, I'm afraid it can linger for days. As you can see, we have welcomed some other travelers."

Lady Audrey made the introductions and both Tom and Evie managed to give small nods of acknowledgment.

She hoped they wouldn't expect a lively conversation from her. She would like nothing better than to soak in a hot bath and sleep the rest of the day away.

Traveling usually wearied her, but the cold weather and the arduous drive had left her exhausted.

"I suspect you might want a cup of tea first. You can all introduce yourselves properly later on. Yes, I think that would be easiest. There'll be plenty of time."

Evie exchanged a glance with Tom. They hadn't discussed what they would do next.

They settled down by the fireplace and, in no time, one of the other unfortunate souls who'd sought refuge at the manor house wove his way around the drawing room and positioned himself between Evie and Tom where he proceeded to tell them his life story.

Mr. Matthew Ashby had traveled from London and his motor car had actually broken down the day before.

"Sir Kenneth and Lady Audrey have been absolutely marvelous," he said. "I had been on my way up north to visit relatives. They took pity on me and invited me over for Christmas. Otherwise, I would have worked right through."

"Is the motor car with the flat tire yours?" Tom asked.

"Yes, that's the one. I blew out the spare and no one can get to a garage. Not in this weather. Luckily, I encountered Miss Cynthia Gallagher and her friend. They helped me push my motor car along the drive. In hindsight, I should have just left it by the side of the road. At the time, I'd been quite relieved not to have crashed into them."

There had to be a way through, Evie thought. It might require traveling at a snail's pace, but at least it would get them moving.

Looking toward the drawing room doors, Evie wondered about the two visitors Sir Kenneth had received. They had looked like police officers. She didn't think they had been seeking refuge. If they had come on business, it would have to be quite serious for them to venture out under these conditions.

"And what do you do, Mr. Ashby?" Tom asked.

"I'm an architect. I work for Brighton and Howsen. Have you heard of them?"

"I'm afraid not."

"We build cottages primarily… It's been quite busy. You know… Since the end of the war. Quite a lot of parcels of land have become available."

Evie knew that had been happening either through the loss of heirs or bad investments. Quite a few landowners had found themselves in dire circumstances and in need of an influx of ready cash so they were forced to part with land that had probably been in their families for hundreds of years.

A young woman dressed in pale shades of brown approached Evie and took the chair next to her. Tucking her light brown hair back, she introduced herself as Miss Cynthia Gallagher.

The young woman who had assisted the architect…

She engaged Evie in conversation, expressing concern over the weather.

"We were on our way to visit nearby villages… You see, I'm a writer and I'm working on a last-minute article about Christmas in small villages for a ladies' magazine," she explained. "Anyhow, we lost our way several times and then, we were driving in that thick fog. Luckily, Martin, that's the photographer traveling with me, noticed the road leading here." Cynthia pointed to a young man standing by the window, his tweed jacket looking sad. "That's him. Mr. Martin Shay."

As they chatted about the dismal weather, Evie kept her eyes on the doors. Sipping her tea, she wondered why she had become so intrigued by Sir Kenneth's visitors.

If the two men had been taking shelter from the weather, the butler would surely have shown them through to the drawing room. Evie then remembered the butler had suggested they'd looked official. Yes, she thought, they had to be policemen.

Glancing at Tom, she saw him nod his head several times. Whatever Mr. Matthew Ashby was saying to him appeared to hold his interest. However, his eyes expressed a slight preoccupied look so she guessed Tom's thoughts were elsewhere.

She decided he had to be thinking about their destination and their eventual return home.

"Lady Audrey and her husband have been marvelous," Miss Cynthia Gallagher said. "I don't know what we would have done without their hospitality. We understand there is a village nearby with two guest houses. Of course, we have no way of getting there."

As Evie set her teacup down, another guest approached.

Mr. John Arthurs had been traveling around the area in search of rare books.

"Is there a huge demand?" Evie asked.

Adjusting his spectacles on a slightly crooked nose, Mr. Arthurs nodded. "Oh, yes. Definitely. Absolutely. Always."

Evie couldn't imagine why anyone would wish to part with their valuable books. One never knew when they might come in handy.

"My most interested buyers are a new breed. They decorate houses and their clients…" Mr. Arthurs chuckled, "wish to establish themselves."

"In what way?" Evie asked.

"They want to appear to have been around for a long time. You know…" he lowered his voice, "new money. I've heard talk of some nouveau riche buying titles."

As Mr. Arthurs told her everything he knew about the book buying business and his clients, Evie stole a few glances around the drawing room.

Did everyone have a similar story? If she had to

contribute a reason for being out and about at this time of the year, what would she say? She and Tom had trekked out on a wild goose chase in search of Christmas decorations carved by the seven-year-old Earl's father? Or would she admit to wanting to trump Tom's gift to Seth?

She hoped no one asked her.

When she'd told Tom she was happy he'd given Seth a pony, she had meant it. However, his thoughtful gift had made her aware of her own inadequate attempt to purchase an appropriate gift for Seth.

She probably needed to see Seth the way others did. As a little boy, rather than as the Earl of Woodridge.

Clearly, she'd taken her responsibilities too seriously. She had to understand he still needed to have fun.

Perhaps the problem lay with not quite understanding her role in his life. Strictly speaking, she was Seth's guardian. Some would say, she played the role of mother. Of course, she could never step into his mother's shoes, but she could be a constant presence in his life. And not necessarily someone who always pressed him to eat his vegetables...

While she had visited him at boarding school and sent him parcels throughout the year, maybe she could do more.

Giving a small nod, Evie decided she would visit him at boarding school more often. Such a simple solution and one Caro would heartily approve of. She sat back to think about Caro's reaction. She would definitely wish to come along...

Evie returned her attention to Mr. Arthurs. He and Miss Cynthia Gallagher were holding a murmured conversation. Seeing the young woman's gaze skate over to a couple sitting apart from everyone else, Evie strained to hear what they were saying.

"They haven't talked with anyone..."

Evie leaned toward Miss Gallagher. "Who are they?"

"Mr. Anthony Rupert and his wife, Mrs. Annabel Rupert. We've been saying their behavior is odd. Here we all are stranded and doing our best to be friendly and they haven't said a word to any of us. I'm beginning to think they feel our company is not good enough."

"Maybe they're shy," Evie suggested.

They both shook their heads.

"Like us, they've been here since yesterday. Our hosts have been gracious enough to treat us like proper house guests. We've all sat down to dinner with them and, I must say, I've never seen such a splendid offering. They have two footmen and a butler." Cynthia's eyes widened. "Two. Can you believe that?"

Evie didn't know if Cynthia thought two footmen were too few or too many. In which case, what would she make of the number of footmen at Halton House?

Evie couldn't say exactly how many there were, but she knew there were more than two.

"Where was I...? Oh, yes. I think they're snobs and I don't mind saying so. I caught Mrs. Rupert actually looking down her nose at me. Just look at the way they are sitting apart from everyone and watching us as if we might suddenly decide to attack them."

Evie thought Cynthia's observations were valid, up to a point. Some people did not do well among strangers.

"I think they're hiding something," the young woman added.

Gesturing to a man sitting in a corner with a book, Evie asked, "Who is he?"

"That's Mr. Hector Hollings. He arrived early this morning. Apparently, he spent the night in his motor car and ended up pushing it all the way here. I think he ran out of fuel. Sir Kenneth said he could help him with that, but it wouldn't do much good in this weather because it would be too dangerous to drive."

Lady Audrey stood in the middle of the drawing room looking around. Making eye contact with Evie, she smiled and walked toward her.

"Lady Woodridge. Luncheon will be at one. Simmons informs me he has taken your luggage to your room. I've sent up a maid to take care of everything for you."

Evie thanked her and apologized for the intrusion.

"Oh, it's no intrusion. In fact, Sir Kenneth and I are always prepared to receive unexpected guests at this time of the year. There are so many more people getting out and about these days. I doubt we'll ever complain of being bored or lonely." Lady Audrey wrung her hands and looked toward the doors.

Either Evie imagined it or her hostess looked worried. She placed her hand to her forehead and turned to Evie.

"Heavens, you might think this odd, but I have the strangest feeling we are about to receive very bad news."

Evie couldn't help raising her eyebrows slightly, not so much at the prospect of hearing bad news but at Lady Audrey's melodramatic tone.

Lady Audrey smiled. "Yes, I know it sounds odd. Sir Kenneth finds it all too amusing but ever since one of our neighbors gave a talk at an afternoon tea about our intuitive faculty, I have been aware of the ability to sense the slightest disturbances in our otherwise happy home."

"Your neighbor sounds interesting," Cynthia remarked.

"Yes, she is. She lives in a farmhouse nearby and is… what we might refer to as a patroness of the arts. Although, Sir Kenneth insists on referring to her as a *bohemian*. She has given refuge to poets, artists and writers who might otherwise live on the streets."

Cynthia Gallagher seemed to find this information surprising. "Surely not in this day and age."

"Perhaps you are too young to have noticed there are people who have no way of avoiding the work-house. Anyhow, Elsbeth is in a position to offer shelter and a means to earn their keep while having time to work at their craft."

"That is highly commendable," Evie offered.

Lady Audrey placed her hand against her throat and shivered. "Did you feel that?"

Evie glanced around her but didn't sense anything.

"The strangest sensation," Lady Audrey added.

The door to the drawing room opened and a distinguished looking gentleman walked in. Glancing around the room, he spotted Lady Audrey and gave her a small nod.

As he made his way toward her, his eyes remained pinned on hers. "My dear, I'm afraid we have received some rather worrying news."

Lady Audrey gasped. "I knew it. How bad is it?"

"Dreadful. You must brace yourself. It's Miles Barton."

Lady Audrey eased herself down onto a chair. "He's dead."

The man Evie assumed was Sir Kenneth Audrey nodded. "Two gentlemen just paid me a visit to deliver the news. They were policemen."

"Were?" Lady Audrey asked.

"Well, I suppose they still are, but they've now left. Anyhow, it appears Miles Barton has died under suspicious circumstances. I will spare you the details."

Lady Audrey gasped again. "Foul means?"

Sir Kenneth nodded again. "I have been warned to beware of strangers."

CHAPTER 5

*T*he butler signaled to Lady Audrey and she said, her tone unexpectedly bright, "I believe lunch is served. Shall we go in?"

The gravity of the news she'd just heard seemed to have been forgotten.

Evie glanced at Tom only to find him already looking at her, his face lit up with surprise.

Beware of strangers?

She had the oddest sensation of being watched by seven pairs of eyes, each one more threatening than the other.

"I have asked the police to keep us informed and they have promised to return in the morning. Although, how they'll manage to get through is anyone's guess," Sir Kenneth said as he made his way out of the drawing room.

Evie wanted to ask if he had told the police he had given shelter to seven strangers. Nine counting herself and Tom. In which case, why would the police not interview them now?

When Tom gave her his arm, he asked, "What happened to the order of precedence?"

"I think, despite appearances, our hosts might both be preoccupied by the news."

"Still, you do hold the highest rank…"

Evie smiled. "Is that why you are always nearby ready to escort me in?"

He shrugged. "First in… and all that jazz."

Evie leaned in and whispered, "So, what do you make of all that?"

"The news about the death or Sir Kenneth and his wife's odd behavior?"

"True. He does seem to be taking it all in his stride. I wonder if we have reason to worry. Do you think…" She didn't dare say it, and she didn't need to.

"I assume you were about to say there might be a killer on the loose, and possibly, a killer staying right here," Tom said. "Yes. Most likely."

"This is one of those moments where hindsight becomes quite educational. Instead of dashing out, I should have asked if you have any woodcarving skills. Heavens, there must be someone working at Halton House with such skills. Oh, why didn't I think of it instead of proposing this mad outing?"

"Since Henrietta is not here to say it, I will." Clearing his throat, Tom surprised Evie by giving an impressive impersonation of the dowager, "Evangeline, you were bound to run into some curious business."

Evie gave an unladylike snort. When she composed herself, she whispered, "Next time you do that, please warn me."

"All right. Brace yourself." This time, Tom impersonated Toodles, "I say, Birdie, what are you going to do about this? How are you going to find the killer?"

Pursing her lips, Evie slanted her gaze at him. "You've been practicing. Can you do me?"

Tom gaped at her.

Evie gaped. "Oh, you are horrid."

"I do my best." Tom leaned in and whispered. "Why do you think the police left? They must have seen the motor cars outside. Surely, they would want to speak with us."

"I entertained the same thought," Evie whispered. "Your guess is as good as mine."

They were led through to an elegant room, the windows facing the park.

Settling down with Tom beside her, Evie looked around the room and noticed the hunting trophies hanging on the walls. She shivered. Boars and deer heads gazed down at them. Evie found their steely gazes discomforting. Even without looking at them, she found it difficult to ignore their presence.

"I hope they don't serve venison," she murmured.

When everyone took their places, Sir Kenneth drew their attention by saying, "Miles Barton moved into the district a couple of years ago. He mostly kept to himself. That makes his death quite puzzling."

"He kept to himself because he had an interest," Lady Audrey chimed in. Looking around the table, she added, "He was a botanist. His studies took him all over the world. I believe he spent some time in America and Australia. His wife didn't care much for all that traveling and has been happy since settling here."

"Was he young?" Cynthia Gallagher asked.

Lady Audrey laughed. "My dear, everyone appears young to us. I suppose he must have been in his early forties. Yes, far too young to have died."

"How did he die?" Cynthia asked.

Glad someone had thought to ask the obvious question, Evie looked down at her plate. The picture of a stag stared right back at her.

When she looked up, she saw everyone leaning slightly forward, their attention fixed on Sir Kenneth, eager to hear his response.

"A severe blow to the back of the head," Sir Kenneth revealed.

No one responded. Not even with a gasp of surprise. Had everyone become impervious to violent deaths?

Two years had passed since the end of the war and

that had been a time when just about everyone Evie knew had received news of a loss. Even those who had been fortunate enough to not lose anyone close to them had suffered from seeing the pain of everyone else's losses. Then there had been the survivors who had suffered from the severe soul numbing shock of their experiences...

The book buyer, Mr. John Arthurs cleared his throat and asked, his tone matter-of-fact, "Do the police suspect someone of delivering the blow?"

Someone harrumphed. "Well, he could hardly have performed the deed himself."

Surprise registered on everyone's face. They all turned toward the person who had spoken.

Mrs. Annabel Rupert.

The snob!

"There's someone who doesn't think much of us," Tom whispered.

"Cynthia Gallagher labeled her a snob," Evie whispered back and gestured across the table to the young woman.

Lady Audrey's sigh drew everyone's attention back to her. "I told Lady Woodridge I sensed something in the air. A disturbance I couldn't quite explain."

The lady of the house looked at Evie as if seeking confirmation.

"I think you are being prompted," Tom whispered.

"Oh, yes. Yes, indeed," Evie offered. She had actually

tried to sense something too but she had still been trying to shake off the cold that had seeped right through to her bones. In any case, she didn't think she had been empowered with any particular sensibilities...

"Events such as this one," Lady Audrey continued, "alter the energy around us."

Sir Kenneth laughed. "My wife is a great believer of the spiritual life and the energy around us all."

Right on cue, everyone looked around as if trying to catch sight of this energy Lady Audrey spoke of.

"Perhaps we should hold a séance," Cynthia suggested.

Lady Audrey looked at her husband who gave her a small nod.

"That could be arranged. Oh... if only... If only we could contact Elsbeth."

"Has she been dead long?" Cynthia asked.

"Oh, no dear. She is quite alive. Elsbeth is a neighbor but she does not own a telephone."

"Elsbeth is a *bohemian*," Sir Kenneth added. "She holds some rather unusual beliefs."

"That's because she is open-minded," Lady Audrey said.

"Is it possible he might have slipped and hit his head?" Mr. Hector Hollings asked. Noticing everyone's attention shift toward him, he adjusted his glasses. "It's been known to happen. I visit many private libraries and have experienced a couple of close calls climbing step ladders. I don't mind admitting I actually took a tumble once. If one were to… lose one's balance, it's feasible one could fall and hit one's head… against the edge of a table."

Tom nudged Evie and whispered, "Are you going to tell them about your experience up a ladder in the library?" Tom nudged her again. "You should at least rescue the man. He looks uncomfortable now. Go on."

Evie knew Tom was teasing her but he had a point. No one had responded to Mr. Hollings' admission and suggestion. His cheeks had colored and he looked as if he wanted the earth to swallow him whole. "Actually, I too have had an experience while climbing a library ladder. They can be perilous. From memory, I nearly cracked open Mr. Winchester's skull with a heavy tome." Evie glanced at Tom and saw him nodding.

"To this day," Evie added, "I believe he might have suffered a concussion. He has occasional bouts of talking gibberish."

"Oh, my goodness," Lady Audrey sent Tom a sympathetic smile.

Tom rubbed his head. "Yes, there are days when I still feel my head throbbing. It usually signals the approach of a storm."

Sir Kenneth laughed. "You would be a handy fellow to have around. No need for a barometer." He turned to his wife and gave her an indulgent smile. "I will see what I can do about bringing Elsbeth here. A séance might be just what we need to distract ourselves."

"Wouldn't it be disrespectful?" the snobbish Mrs. Rupert asked, her tone hard.

"I don't see why," Cynthia said. "The poor man is probably trying to contact someone even as we speak. He might be able to tell us something about his killer."

Once again, everyone looked around them.

"What if it's one of us?"

Everyone, including Evie and Tom looked from one guest to the other trying to identify the person who had spoken.

The only one not looking around was Mr. Hector Hollings, who went on to say, "The police have warned Sir Kenneth to be wary of strangers."

"What utter nonsense," the snobbish Mrs. Rupert clipped out.

"When was he killed, Sir Kenneth?" Cynthia asked.

"The police were not clear about that. However, they said they were called in during the night."

"So it could not have been one of us. We were all here," Cynthia reasoned.

"That's not quite true," Evie whispered.

"What makes you say that?" Tom asked.

"I'll tell you later." Evie remembered Cynthia saying Mr. Hollins had arrived that morning. His motor car had run out of fuel… Had he been trying to make his escape?

"Well, in any case, the police will return. They have asked me to provide them with your names." Sir Kenneth looked around the table. "I hope no one objects."

The footmen began setting the first course plates down.

Thick soup, with plenty of vegetables. A hearty meal to ward off the cold. Evie savored the first spoonful and sighed with contentment, the unfortunate death all but forgotten.

"Sir Kenneth, please excuse my writer's curiosity," Cynthia said. "Is there anything else you can tell us about the victim?"

Sir Kenneth turned to his butler. "Simmons, have you heard anything interesting about Miles Barton?"

"I can't say that I have, Sir Kenneth."

Sir Kenneth grunted. "That means he ran a happy household. If there had been anything odd about the man, the servants would have spread the word. That's why we try to keep Simmons and the rest of the staff happy. We wouldn't want everyone finding out about our oddities. Lady Audrey and myself can be... odd fish at times. Ask Simmons about me swimming in the lake in my birth suit and he will deny it until he is blue in the face."

Lady Audrey laughed. "Simmons won't have to deny it now, dear. You've just informed all our guests."

"There's nothing finer than a dip in the lake," Sir

Kenneth declared. "Even in the dead of winter. It strengthens one's constitution."

Evie leaned in and whispered, "Remind me to pay special attention to the staff's Christmas gifts this year."

"Why? Have you been swimming in the lake naked?"

Cynthia and Mr. Hollings continued to toss around speculative ideas about the killer's identity.

At one point, Evie suspected she and Tom had been targeted as possible suspects. After all, they too had arrived that morning.

"We might need to work on our alibis," Tom whispered. "We are, after all, the most likely suspects. I wouldn't be surprised if they post a guard outside our doors."

"How long do you think we'll be here?" At some point, she would need to telephone Halton House and let them know of their delay, but Evie feared that might worry everyone.

"This is a dreadful tragedy," Lady Audrey exclaimed. "We must find a way to reach the house. Eleanor Barton must be beside herself with grief." She gave a firm nod. "She's not the friendliest soul but no one should be left alone in their hour of need."

"Please don't fret. I will do what I can," Sir Kenneth assured his wife.

Evie reached for her wine glass and whispered, "That means there is a way out."

"The house is probably within walking distance," Tom suggested. "Sir Kenneth shouldn't have any difficulty finding his way and he'll have someone with him. A gamekeeper or someone else acquainted with the area."

"Do you suppose… we might go along with him?"

CHAPTER 6

"You didn't answer my question," Evie said as they settled into the library. Out of all the guests staying at Sir Kenneth's house, they were the only two who had chosen to spend the afternoon among books. Everyone else had opted to while away the time in the drawing room playing cards, with the snobbish Mrs. Rupert choosing to entertain herself with a game of solitaire while her husband looked on in silence.

"Why do you wish to go out in this weather?" Tom asked.

Evie fished around for a solid reason. "I suspect Miles Barton lived in the house owned by Seth's parents. Sir Kenneth mentioned Mr. Barton had only moved to the district two years ago."

"You could confirm the address with Sir Kenneth."

Yes, she could. But if it turned out to be a different house, then there would be no need to go along with Sir Kenneth.

Tom stood by a table sifting through a stack of newspapers.

"I see Sir Kenneth is a hoarder."

"Yes," Tom said. "The latest newspaper is dated two days ago. I suppose that's when the delivery stopped because of the fog. Oh... Look at this."

Evie went to stand beside him.

"It's an advertisement," he said. "This might be that lady detective Toodles has been talking about."

London's Foremost Lady Detective.

"Well, that's that. I can't possibly turn my attention to becoming a lady detective. She has already staked her claim."

"Really? But you're a *real* Lady." Tom laughed. "You could be the One and *Only* Lady Detective."

"You know very well I can't exploit my title in such a manner. It would be an abuse of my privilege. Henrietta would never allow it."

He turned the page. "Well, well. It seems there is already some sort of competition happening. Here is another advertisement by another woman detective, and she claims to be London's Leading Woman in Every Branch of Detective Work."

"There, that says it all. It would be foolish to compete with two seasoned female detectives." Evie shook her head. "No, I don't wish to come between two women already jostling for attention."

Tom hummed under his breath. "With the rise in divorce cases, there must be an increase in demand for incriminating evidence."

"I'm not so sure about that," Evie mused. "Divorce is still relatively new and available only to those who can afford it and most gentlemen are prepared to provide the proof themselves."

"You seem to be quite knowledgeable on the subject."

Evie gave a casual shrug. "I've heard a rumor or two."

"And how exactly does the gentleman provide proof?" Tom asked.

Evie pressed her finger on the table and drew a circle. "Apparently, arrangements are made, assignations organized and a photographer employed to catch the couple *in flagrante delicto*. Of course, the lady is someone merely employed to pose as the guilty party. In any case, I doubt I would want to become involved in divorce proceedings. It all seems so sordid."

"I suppose you would prefer a good old-fashioned murder case."

Evie nodded. "Only because I am intrigued by people's motives. You must admit, we have encountered some odd creatures as well as some vile ones."

Tom picked up another newspaper. He turned several pages. "Here's a picture of her."

The photograph looked grainy. "She could be anyone from our local village."

"How would you describe her?"

"Regular, nondescript features." She looked closer. "There really isn't anything about her that stands out. Put a wig on her and she could be anyone. Put an apron on her and she could be a cook. Put a feather hat on her and… she could be my great aunt, Louella." She clicked her fingers. "That's another reason why I couldn't be a lady detective. No matter how I dressed, I'd still be recognized as myself."

She watched Tom turn to the obituaries page. "He won't be listed," Evie said.

"Oh, I wasn't looking for Miles Barton's name. If you went into the detective business, it might be worth your while checking the obituaries. Something might catch your eye. After all, you move in certain circles so an unexpected death might pique your curiosity."

"Are you now suggesting I chase after murder and intrigue?"

"Why not? News reporters chase after news and when they can't find it, they… become creative."

Evie crossed her arms. "No one has bothered to ask the obvious question. So, I'll go ahead and answer it. I am happy being the Countess of Woodridge."

"Be honest. Sometimes, you're happy to answer the call to adventure."

Evie harrumphed. "I know what you're trying to do."

"Enlighten me."

"You are trying to distract me from thinking about Sir Kenneth's visit to Miles Barton's house."

Tom laughed.

"I see, you are amused."

"Yes, by this…" Tom tapped his finger on a page. "Revolver shot at séance. Lady detective to shoot spirit."

"That sounds intriguing. She must have performed some sort of undercover work. What else does it say?"

"She had been trying to unmask a fraud. Looks like this lady detective enjoys attracting attention to herself as a way of advertising her services. That's something you could definitely do, without even trying." He tipped his head back, closed his eyes, and laughed.

"Now what?"

"I'm now picturing Caro in tow. She would do everything in her power to ensure you did not tarnish your reputation." Tom cleared his throat and mimicked Caro. "Milady, you have been presented."

Tapping her foot, Evie gave him a small smile. "Oh, yes. I can picture it too. And I don't even need to close my eyes to see you in the thick of it too."

The doors to the library opened and the butler walked in carrying a tray with a teapot and two cups. "Lady Audrey thought you might enjoy some refreshments, my lady."

"Thank you, Simmons. Are these all the newspapers you have?"

"Yes, my lady. The boy from the village has used the fog as an excuse to stop all deliveries."

Did that mean the boy suffered from lethargy or did he have some other reason for avoiding the house?

"How does he usually travel here?" Evie asked.

"He bicycles in. There's an old road leading to the village. Even by motor car, it takes twice as long to travel through but it's on higher ground, so the fog doesn't affect it."

Evie glanced at Tom and wondered how amenable he would be to trying this road out.

"Sir Kenneth will travel along it tomorrow," Simmons continued. "He has already requested the carriage to be readied."

"Carriage?"

"Sir Kenneth is never in any hurry to get anywhere and so he has not embraced the new transportation modes. He prefers to get around in a horse drawn carriage. The barouche is his favorite. He has quite a collection of them, among them, a perfectly maintained Hansom cab."

"I wonder if Sir Kenneth would enjoy some company," Evie mused loud enough to be heard by Simmons.

"If you like, I could express your desire to join him, my lady. He will be traveling in a closed carriage."

"Oh… if it isn't inconvenient, of course."

"It would be my pleasure, my lady." The butler turned to leave.

"Simmons," Tom called out.

"Yes, sir?"

"Did I just detect a sign of relief from you?"

"Pardon?"

"You looked somewhat grateful to hear her ladyship express an interest in traveling with Sir Kenneth in the carriage," Tom said, leaving no room for confusion.

Simmons looked toward the windows and shivered. "I'm afraid I do not share Sir Kenneth's robust constitution."

"Otherwise, you would be traveling with him?"

"For some reason, Sir Kenneth rather enjoys my company."

Tom thanked him for the information and waited for him to leave before saying, "Surely, you're not seriously thinking of going along."

Evie gasped. "Oh, I just remembered what I was going to tell you earlier on."

"Are you trying to change the subject?"

Not intentionally, Evie thought. However, she found herself feeling quite thrilled by the possibility of doing so. She always seemed to be at the receiving end of people changing the subject... "It's about Cynthia Gallagher."

"You *are* trying to change the subject."

"Do you want to hear what I have to say, or not?"

Tom sat down.

Huzzah! Evie savored her moment of triumph. Finally, she had managed to divert Tom's attention.

"I believe Cynthia has told a little white lie." Evie walked over to the table. "Tea?"

"Yes, please."

Evie poured the tea and took the cup over to him.

"You were saying?" he encouraged.

"Oh..." She looked up at the ceiling.

"Are you trying to be evasive again?" Tom asked.

"Why would I do that?"

He quirked an eyebrow.

Smiling, she walked back to the table to pour herself a cup of tea. "Matthew Ashby said he'd been lucky he hadn't collided with Cynthia. That suggests—" hearing the door to the library opening, Evie broke off.

"Oh, here you are." Cynthia Gallagher walked in

and went to stand by the fireplace. "Why am I not surprised to find you both in the library?"

Evie had no idea. Nothing she'd said would have suggested they took a keen interest in books.

Mouthing an apology to Tom for the unexpected interruption, she said, "I'd offer you some tea but I'm afraid there are only two cups."

Cynthia smiled. "Thank you, but I think I've had my fill of tea for today. We have all been drinking copious amounts of it in the drawing room."

Tom set his cup down and looked toward the windows. Mirroring him, Evie saw what had drawn his attention. A handsome looking carriage drawn by two horses drove by. "Oh, I wonder where he is going."

"I heard Sir Kenneth say he would do what he could to convince his neighbor, Elsbeth, to come to the house tonight," Cynthia said. "I suspect that might be an estate worker on his way to collect her. I do hope she is willing to come out in this weather."

"It should be interesting," Evie mused. "I have never attended a séance."

"I have. At least, I think I have."

"What makes you doubt it?" Evie asked.

"I attended a couple, but after witnessing it all, I still remain somewhat skeptical. There have been numerous so-called mediums exposed as charlatans out to exploit people's vulnerabilities. I had to write an article on the subject of séances. They became quite the rage after the war with those wishing to contact their loved ones. I couldn't bring myself to throw too much doubt on the practice because I could see the comfort the experience offered to those seeking assurances that their loved ones were happy."

"How could you tell a fraud from a genuine medium?"

"Some use stage magic, illusion and a number of dubious means. There was a recent case of a lady detective engaged by a woman who told her she needed information on another woman. She asked the detective to leave the information in a sealed envelope at a certain address. The detective became suspicious when the address given to her turned out to be a store where people collected mail. She followed her client who turned out to be a society fortune-teller."

"I see. So, a medium could collect information on the deceased and pass it on as a message from the great beyond."

"Precisely. Then, there are stage props. Little tricks used to make tables levitate."

"That could not possibly happen here." Looking toward the window at the disappearing carriage, Evie added, "Oh, I do hope Lady Audrey's neighbor agrees to come. I am now quite looking forward to the experience. How exactly is it conducted?"

"They usually take place in a semi-dark room."

Cynthia looked around the library and gave a small nod. "We'll need a round table."

"Is that essential?"

"The idea is to have a number of people form a circle."

The door to the library opened again and Martin Shay stepped forward. Seeing Evie and Tom, Cynthia's friend went no further. "If I could have a word with you, please," he said.

Excusing herself, Cynthia left.

After a moment, Tom prompted Evie. "You were saying…"

"I wonder what that was all about?"

"I think Ms. Gallagher might have tired of the company in the drawing room. Now…" he sat up. "You were about to tell me something."

"Matthew Ashby said he was on his way to visit his family for Christmas and he hails from London. How could he have nearly collided with Cynthia Gallagher and Martin Shay? They were all headed in the same direction."

Tom appeared to think about it for a moment and then he stood up. "Did we assume Cynthia and her photographer friend, Martin, were also headed north?"

"I think we did."

"So one of them is lying."

"Presumably. I'm quite sure Matthew said he'd risked colliding head on with Cynthia's motor car."

Evie held up a finger. "Wait a minute. I think Cynthia said they got lost. Maybe that explains why they were on a collision course. They must have doubled back."

"But, if one of them is lying, then one of them might have been coming back from the direction of the village."

"Yes… That's the idea I'd been entertaining. The police suspect foul play. If the killer happened to be forced off the road by a thick fog, they might want to hide the fact they had just come from the village."

Tom ran his finger along the rim of the cup. "It will be interesting to hear what they say to the police. If Matthew Ashby began his journey from London, what was he doing on this road?"

"Perhaps he took the scenic route," Evie suggested.

"Or…"

"Or?"

"He lied about going up north to visit family. Either that, or he has a hopeless sense of direction."

CHAPTER 7

*R*etiring to her room for an hour before dinner gave Evie the opportunity to settle down and accept the fact she and Tom were stuck in the house, for the time being, at least.

They could now both claim to be intimately familiar with Sir Kenneth's library. Tom had been happy to spend most of his time reading his way through the stack of newspapers available, while Evie had perused the shelves, occasionally pulling out a book for closer inspection. One book in particular had caught her eye. The Great Boer War, written by Arthur Conan Doyle, an author she had become familiar with after reading some of his Sherlock Holmes books. She had managed to read through the first few chapters and now had a better understanding of how that particular war had started.

If she happened to encounter an awkward moment in conversation, she could always bring up the subject. Or, she could store the information for future use. It would certainly come in handy as a diversionary tactic...

Evie smiled. Her granny would think it a great subject to use in order to get rid of someone she didn't wish to speak with.

A knock at her door had her stepping back from the window. She shifted her gaze away from the white landscape and called out, "Come in."

Lady Audrey walked in, her mop of blonde curls tamed by a colorful scarf, tied at the side and cascading down to her shoulder. "I hope I'm not interrupting."

"Not at all. I was just admiring your park. It looks magical in the fading light."

"Oh, yes. I never tire of looking at it. Every season introduces a new palette. I couldn't pick a favorite one, not even if my life depended on it."

Evie watched as Lady Audrey held her hands clasped into a tight ball. She looked flustered. "Is there something worrying you?" Evie asked. Something other than the possibility of a killer being under her roof, she thought. Evie only then realized she had taken the news with the calmness of someone used to dealing with such matters.

"I'm glad you asked. As a matter of fact... I wondered if you might refrain from changing for dinner tonight. The other guests don't have the appropriate clothes—"

Smiling, Evie said, "I will come as I am. Mr. Winchester and I are quite used to adapting to unusual circumstances."

"Thank goodness. One never knows. I for one wouldn't care if we all settled in the drawing room to enjoy a picnic spread out on the floor."

"That would be fun."

"Yes, I think so too, but I'm afraid Simmons is set in his ways. Heaven only knows what he'll make of tonight's séance. That is, if Elsbeth agrees to come. I'll see you downstairs shortly." Lady Audrey shivered.

"Oh, did you just have a premonition?" Evie asked.

Lady Audrey raised her eyebrows in surprise. "Premonition? No, I just felt a draft." She turned to leave only to stop. "Although... This room has always felt odd. It's those vibes. They're all over the place..."

Evie watched her leave and stood in the middle of the room looking around. While reluctant to criticize her hostess, in Evie's opinion, one did not hint at the possibility of a room being haunted and then leave...

Stifling a yelp, she hurried out of the room and bumped into Tom.

"In a hurry?" he asked.

"I've decided we will take our chances tomorrow and follow Sir Kenneth to his neighbor's house."

Tom slipped his hands inside his pockets. "I suppose there is no point in trying to talk you out of it."

"I'm prepared to listen to any reasonable arguments against the idea but you should know I will also want to hear a long list of alternatives. We can't possibly stay here forever."

The edge of his lip quivered for a moment. Tom appeared to struggle to keep a straight face, but then his lips quirked up. "And yet, something tells me I could propose a solution for finding the Christmas decorations and heading back home tonight and you would find a way to delay our departure because you are keen to take part in the séance."

"Oh, yes," Evie chirped. "That goes without saying. Although…" Evie looked over her shoulder. "Did you sense anything in your room?"

"No, it's perfectly comfortable," he said. "Although, Lady Audrey just had one of her experiences when she came by to ask that I refrain from changing into formal clothes for dinner."

"I see. She is making the rounds and spreading her fear."

"Fear?" Tom laughed. "She might actually be trying to set the mood for tonight's séance."

"Oh. I hadn't thought of that. Well, that makes her rather an accomplished hostess."

As they made their way along the hallway, they stopped to admire the paintings of distant ancestors.

"My goodness. This one is dressed in Elizabethan clothes. Sir Kenneth's family must go back a long way."

"Just imagine all those travelers who found their way to this house," Tom said. "They might be the ones haunting our rooms."

Evie slipped her arm through his and tugged him along. "I have just discovered I have a vivid imagination. It will do me no good tonight when I try to fall asleep."

He laughed. "So you can actually picture those ghosts reaching out to you?"

Evie hurried her step. "Now I'm picturing you as a little boy, relentlessly teasing little girls."

Tom grinned. "I've spent many years honing my skills."

"Heavens, and you're not even denying it."

They found everyone gathered in the drawing room enjoying drinks before dinner. Sir Kenneth stood by the fireplace holding a large glass and having a lively conversation with Cynthia Gallagher.

To Evie's surprise, the snooty couple, Mr. and Mrs. Rupert, were seated together with Cynthia's friend, Martin Shay. However, they were all staring into space and not talking.

"Ah, Lady Woodridge." The book buyer, John Arthurs, claimed Evie's attention.

Tom excused himself and made his way to speak with Matthew Ashby. Evie hoped he remembered to ask a few pertinent questions to determine if Mr. Ashby had been driving away or toward the village.

"How did you find Sir Kenneth's library?" John Arthurs asked.

"It's impressive but a large number of books will always impress me." She smiled. "They appeared to be well read."

"That's quite an observation." Mr. Arthurs adjusted his glasses on his nose. "Take it from someone who spends a lot of time in libraries, not all books are read."

Evie tried to remember if he had given any specific information about his job. "This is a strange time of the year to be out and about searching for books."

"I quite agree. Yes, indeed. However, I'm at the mercy of people's whims."

"I'm surprised anyone is willing to part with rare books."

"It's not always by choice," he said and looked around him. Lowering his voice, he asked, "What do you think of this business?"

"The séance?"

"No, the death. Do you think the person responsible might be among us?"

Evie couldn't tell if he had wanted to shift the focus away from talking about books or if he really wished to discuss Miles Barton's death. "Anything is possible." Evie glanced at Mr. and Mrs. Rupert. They remained seated in silence with Martin Shay. Another sweep of the drawing room revealed Sir Kenneth still engaged in conversation with Cynthia Gallagher but they had now been joined by Mr. Hector Hollings. Evie wondered what the police would make of his arrival in the morning after Miles Barton's death. It would be interesting to find out if he had been headed toward the village or away...

"You don't sound concerned," the book buyer said.

"I doubt the killer will try anything foolish. I'm sure the killer is eager to get away with his crime. That is usually the case." Before he could question her knowledge of such matters, Evie tilted her head and asked, "So, are you after a particular book?"

He gave a small nod. "Indeed. Oh, yes. Yes, indeed." Adjusting his glasses, he leaned in. "It's a twelfth-century manuscript. Much sought after. The owner is actually keen to sell and I am equally keen to buy."

So, she had been wrong about him wanting to change the subject. Evie had seen a few manuscripts with hand painted images. She realized this most likely meant it pre-dated the printing press. "Who would sell something so valuable?" She laughed. "Of course. Someone in need of the income."

"Strangely, that is not always the case," he said. "Some people inherit estates and have no appreciation for such things so they are more than willing to part with them."

Evie pictured Mr. Arthurs rubbing his hands with glee and anticipation.

"I hope you don't mind me asking." His eyes lit up. "Do you happen to have any surplus books you wish to find a good home for?"

"That is such a pleasant way of asking." Evie smiled. "Unfortunately for you, we treasure our collection."

"If I may…" He handed Evie a business card.

"I will keep you in mind if I happen to hear of anyone wishing to sell or buy books-."

"That is very gracious of you, my lady. If you'll excuse me, I'd like to have a glimpse of Sir Kenneth's library. I've been waiting for the right moment when I could have the place to myself."

Evie patted her skirt, but didn't find a pocket, so she edged toward Tom and slipped the business card into his pocket.

Sensing her, Tom turned. "We were just discussing the perils of driving in this weather."

"Without a spare tire, I don't really have a choice," Matthew Ashby said. "I might end up trying to get to the train station."

Evie assumed he would get there in one of Sir Kenneth's carriages…

"You're not drinking, my lady?" Matthew Ashby asked.

Just then, Simmons approached with a tray.

"Thank you, Simmons." It seemed Sir Kenneth

believed in only offering two types of drink; whiskey or gin. Evie took a tumbler of whiskey.

Tom leaned in and said, "Before we got onto the subject of motor cars, we discussed the possibility of one of us being the killer. Matthew also expressed surprise at the police not interviewing us today."

"They might be busy chasing the real culprit," Evie reasoned, and thought to add, "In the fog."

"Or maybe Sir Kenneth knows something we don't," Tom suggested.

Evie looked toward Sir Kenneth. "I'm sure Sir Kenneth would not subject his guests to any danger."

Matthew Ashby laughed. "Perhaps Lady Audrey has consulted with the vibrations in her house and they have assured her we are all harmless."

Just then, Lady Audrey entered the drawing room, went to stand in the middle of the drawing room and clapped her hands. "If I could have everyone's attention, please."

Mrs. Rupert pursed her lips and lifted her chin as if readying herself to cast her strongest objections to whatever Lady Audrey wished to announce.

"I would like to introduce our wonderful friend and neighbor, Elsbeth, who has agreed to guide us in our attempt to contact the spirits."

Evie watched for anyone rolling their eyes, but apart from Mrs. Rupert who managed a slight lift of her eyebrows, everyone appeared to be intrigued by the prospect of engaging with the great beyond.

A woman stepped forward. Tall and slim, she wore her dark hair unfashionably long, the locks tamed by a colorful head scarf. Her dark eyes sparkled with hidden knowledge and her warm smile seemed to promise only kind words for everyone.

Lady Audrey took her around the room and introduced her to everyone. Before she could get to Evie, a commotion startled the guests.

The doors to the drawing room burst open and a woman dressed in a fur lined winter coat rushed in.

"I must insist you put a stop to this nonsense at once."

CHAPTER 8

"My dear Mrs. Barton," Lady Audrey exclaimed, her voice filled with surprise and concern. She looked at her husband as if seeking guidance but he looked equally stunned by the widow's sudden appearance and outburst.

The *bohemian*, Elsbeth, acted with swift promptness and rushed toward the recently widowed woman, placing a comforting arm around her shoulders. "Eleanor. I thought you said you didn't wish to participate in the seance. Did you change your mind?"

Evie strained to hear the woman's response but her soft voice didn't travel across the room. Only moments before she had barged in with the fierceness of a lioness and now she appeared to have lost her bravado. Her eyes widened and she looked about the drawing room as if only now noticing the other people in there.

"Mrs. Barton is clearly upset. That should tell you something. This is wrong. We shouldn't be dabbling with things that don't concern us."

One by one, everyone turned toward Mrs. Rupert. Determined to voice her objections, she continued, "It's plain wrong. You should all be ashamed of yourselves, having fun at someone else's expense."

"My dear Mrs. Rupert, I can assure you we had no such intention." Lady Audrey turned to the widow, her hands pressed together in supplication. "I am so sorry if this has distressed you, Mrs. Barton. We don't even know if it will work. After all, there is quite a distance between our houses."

"Distance has no bearing on such matters, Lady Audrey." Elsbeth guided Mrs. Barton to a chair and signaled to Simmons who didn't need further prompting to deliver a glass of whisky.

"You are in shock," Elsbeth said. "You know this will bring you closure. It's only been a day. Think about it. How will you feel if you miss out? In a day or two, you will come to regret it." Elsbeth looked up at Lady Audrey. "As a matter of fact, Lady Audrey, we can only benefit from Eleanor Barton's presence. Miles Barton loved her a great deal and has no doubt followed her here."

Evie shivered.

"Do you really think so?" Lady Audrey asked.

"Of course, he has," Sir Kenneth's voice boomed

across the drawing room. "The man understood his obligations. He might have been a recluse and took no interest in the sporting life, shunning shooting and horse riding, but I'm sure he would do everything in his power to offer his wife some sort of comfort. No doubt he wishes to impart some final words to his beloved. So, just as well you came, Mrs. Barton. Without your presence, he might have been reluctant to appear to us."

Evie studied the woman. If she engaged her in conversation, Mrs. Barton would need to stand on her toes to reach Evie's shoulders. She had honey-blonde locks peeking out from under a prim hat, large brown eyes and a wide mouth.

When she'd burst into the drawing room, her eyes had been hard, but as Elsbeth offered her some comforting words, they softened.

"I'd like to know how she managed to trek out here," Evie murmured.

"I think I heard a motor car," Matthew Ashby said. "Mrs. Barton must have taken that road Sir Kenneth spoke of."

Evie glanced at Tom.

"I suppose you will insist on going to the village tomorrow," Tom said. "Keep in mind, Sir Kenneth no longer has a need to visit Mrs. Barton. We will be on our own."

"Yes, I will insist on going," Evie declared. "We

cannot afford to linger here any longer than we have to. Delaying our return home will only give rise to suspicion."

Tom tried to hide his smile behind his glass. "Are you saying you don't want Henrietta to find out about any of this?"

Henrietta or her granny, Evie thought. "They would only want to know what I did to find the culprit."

"Are you a lady detective?" Matthew Ashby asked.

"Heavens, no."

"Lady Woodridge is far too modest," Tom said. "She has actually played a major role in discovering the identity of several killers."

"With your assistance," Evie said.

"Oh, I'm merely your sidekick."

"How fascinating." Matthew Ashby glanced at Mrs. Barton. "I say, wouldn't it be interesting if this séance goes ahead and the deceased manages to communicate the identity of his killer."

It would be even more interesting if the killer turned out to be Mrs. Barton, Evie thought. In fact…

Evie shook her head. Her focus should be on sympathizing with the poor woman who had lost her husband and not on accusing her of a grievous crime.

Simmons must have given Lady Audrey a nod. She turned to everyone gathered in the drawing room and announced dinner. "Do please join us, Mrs. Barton."

The widow exchanged a look with Elsbeth and then gave a small nod.

"That's a relief," Matthew Ashby said. "I'm keen to see what happens at a séance. We have to assume there won't be any tricks."

They all began making their way to the dining room in no particular order.

"Elsbeth must live near Mrs. Barton," Evie remarked.

"What makes you say so?" Tom asked.

"Something she said about Mrs. Barton changing her mind. We know Elsbeth doesn't have a telephone. Yet, Mrs. Barton knew about the séance."

Tom nodded. "And she held strong enough opinions to compel her to leave her house, only hours after her husband's death."

"Well, she's changed her mind now. But that's not surprising. People react to a sudden death in different ways. I have a friend who, after learning of her husband's death, decided she needed to go out and organize a whole new set of clothes for herself. Hours later, she sunk into a deep depression and did not emerge from it until several years later. Having lost her husband to drink, she then became a strong proponent of prohibition."

They entered the dining room and were encouraged to sit wherever they wanted to.

The widow and Elsbeth sat at one end. Evie saw

everyone steering clear of them and that left two places.

If given the choice, Evie would have preferred to keep her distance so she could observe and exchange her opinions with Tom.

Gesturing to him, they made their way to sit beside Mrs. Barton.

Evie introduced herself and offered her condolences to the widow.

"Lady Woodridge?" Mrs. Barton studied her for a moment, before asking, "Of Halton House?"

"Yes."

Instead of explaining how she had made the connection, Mrs. Barton lowered her head and then turned to Elsbeth.

"What was that about?" Tom whispered.

"I don't know."

"Perhaps your reputation has preceded you."

"How can that be? My name is always kept out of the papers."

"The rumor mills. Word of mouth, spreading from village to village." Tom laughed.

The footmen began serving the first course. She heard one say it was Oxtail Soup. When she saw Tom cringe, she leaned in and said, "You won't find an actual oxtail in it. I believe it's only used for the stock."

"That's a relief."

Their meals were served. This time, Evie saw Tom

studying the dish. "I guess I was wrong. There are small pieces of oxtail."

"Please stop saying the word oxtail."

Evie couldn't help herself. "I take it you're not comfortable with eating the tail of an ox."

To her surprise, Mrs. Barton followed the usual protocol of turning to the person sitting next to her.

She began by saying, "My husband and I visited Halton House a couple of years ago. He wished to peruse some of your books."

Evie had no recollection of the visit so she assumed she had been abroad at the time. "I hope your visit was fruitful."

"Oh, yes. When not traveling, Miles…my husband, spent his life in libraries."

Evie expected her to turn to Elsbeth and resume whatever conversation they'd been having.

Instead, Mrs. Barton studied Evie for a moment and then said, "I believe there is another connection. When we visited Halton House, we had been on our way to our new house here. A while later, my neighbors informed me the previous tenant had died a few short months before. He had a son. I believe he is now the Earl of Woodridge."

Surprised by the news, Evie turned to Tom. "Did you hear that?"

"I caught most of it, yes. How astonishing."

Evie said, "Mr. Winchester and I had been on our

way to your house. Well, we still are." She told Mrs. Barton about their search for the Christmas decorations.

"You might be in luck," Mrs. Barton said. "I seem to recall Stevens, my butler, mentioning something about finding some boxes. He might know something about them." Mrs. Barton turned her attention to her soup. After a moment, she turned to Elsbeth.

Evie whispered, "We're in luck."

"I hope you don't suggest following her home tonight."

"Have you lost your sense of adventure?"

"I'd like to think I have gained a great deal of common sense."

"I wouldn't dream of suggesting we trek out tonight." In fact, Evie wouldn't be surprised if Lady Audrey insisted Mrs. Barton and Elsbeth spent the night here.

Lady Audrey's cook had to be congratulated. It could not have been easy for her to suddenly have to cook for an extra nine people. Even if they had the occasional unexpected guest, she must be quite a talented cook to be able to produce such consistently delectable dishes.

Conversation flowed but no one broached the subject of the séance. Perhaps in deference to Mrs. Barton's sensitivities.

She had a surprisingly good appetite, eating everything presented to her.

Mrs. Barton looked up and smiled. "Elsbeth has convinced me to participate in the séance."

"Have you attended one before?" The moment the words left her mouth, Evie wished to retrieve them. It almost sounded as if she wanted to know if she made a habit of losing husbands and then trying to contact them.

"Yes, I have. Out of sheer curiosity, I went along to one of Elsbeth's evenings at home." She lowered her voice and added, "She has all those interesting people living with her. Artists and writers. It's not exactly my usual milieu. Everyone seems to be so knowledgeable on just about any subject."

"Did your husband go along with you?"

"Oh, no. Miles had a good laugh about it. He found the whole idea amusing. That's why I don't really think tonight's séance will work."

Evie smiled at the footman as he set a dessert down in front of her.

She heard Mrs. Barton say, "Trifle with glacé cherries. My favorite." She tried it and gave a nod of approval and continued, "My husband didn't have much time for mingling with the local society. He devoted all his time to his studies and observations."

"I heard he traveled a great deal," Evie said.

"Yes, to faraway places. Unfortunately, they held no interest for me. I prefer village life."

To Evie, it sounded as if they had been mismatched.

When the ladies left the gentlemen to their brandy and cigars, Evie found herself once again seated next to Mrs. Barton, while Cynthia Gallagher claimed the space on the other side of the sofa.

Lady Audrey said, "I have given Simmons instructions to set up a round table in the library. We might not all be able to fit in but there will be ample room to spread around. If there is anyone who does not wish to participate, please feel free to remain here."

No one spoke up.

Accepting a cup of coffee, Evie thought she would not miss the experience for anything. She stirred some sugar into her coffee and looked around the drawing room. Elsbeth sat in a corner, her eyes closed. Evie imagined the woman putting herself in the right frame of mind to tackle the spirit world. Mrs. Rupert sat near the fireplace, her attention peeled on the door. Her husband had remained behind with the other gentlemen. Evie considered approaching her and trying to engage her in conversation, but then she decided against it. Instead, she sat back and amused herself with watching Mrs. Rupert staring at the door with fixed determination.

A moment later, she heard Cynthia murmur, "It must have been horrendous for you, Mrs. Barton."

Evie gave up watching Mrs. Rupert and glanced at the widow in time to see her eyes shimmer.

Mrs. Barton gave a pensive nod. "I went down to his office to urge him to put away his work and retire for the night. He had been busy for months after his recent trip to South America."

"And that's when you saw him..." Cynthia prompted.

Mrs. Barton scooped in a breath and shivered. "The police think he might have been attacked from behind. Our butler assured me he had checked all the windows and doors."

"Did the police question all the staff?" Cynthia asked.

"Yes, although... They were all in shock."

"If someone meant to kill him, they must have a motive." Cynthia looked at Evie. "Don't you agree, Lady Woodridge?"

"It might have been a robbery gone wrong," Evie offered. She made a note to contact Detective O'Neill at a future date and ask him if the seasons influenced people with the intention to commit a robbery. Winter didn't strike her as the most convenient time. With snow covering the ground in most parts of the country, there would be footprints...

"They must have asked you some very difficult questions," Cynthia said.

"Oh, yes. Unfortunately, I had no answers for them.

They were interested to know if Miles had any enemies. Well, how could he when he led such a private, quiet life?"

"What did he do?" Cynthia asked.

The question struck Evie as odd because Lady Audrey had already told everyone Mr. Miles Barton had worked as a botanist.

Did botanists have rivals?

"My husband had a keen interest in plants. He traveled a great deal collecting specimens and cataloguing them. He lived in hope of discovering a new species and having it named after himself."

Evie tossed around the information. Traveling around required money so she guessed Miles Barton must have been wealthy enough to support his interest.

"Will you stay on in the district?"

The widow nodded. "I enjoy a quiet life. Although, the house might prove to be too large for me."

A groan had everyone looking up and around the drawing room.

Cynthia Gallagher leaned toward Evie and whispered, "I think Elsbeth has made some sort of contact."

The *bohemian* sprung upright, drew in a deep breath and stretched her arms out. After a moment, she gave a firm nod and opened her eyes. "I do believe we will make contact tonight."

Lady Audrey pressed a hand to her throat. "Oh, dear me. I believe I felt it."

It?

"I didn't feel anything. Did you, Lady Woodridge?" Cynthia asked.

"I'm afraid not. I hope that doesn't have a negative impact on the séance. I should hate to be the one to ruin it for Lady Audrey."

A loud crash had everyone simultaneously jumping to their feet. Silence followed. Everyone stood without moving or saying anything.

Someone behind Evie shifted. She heard an intake of breath and thought they might say something. Wishing to offer some sort of encouragement, Evie turned only to find the space behind her empty.

CHAPTER 9

*T*om entered the drawing room ahead of the other gentlemen. Seeing Evie's stunned expression, he crossed the room. "What happened?"

Evie barely moved her lips when she said, "I'm not sure."

He wrapped his fingers around her arm. "You're as stiff as a board and as white as a sheet." He must have signaled the butler for a drink. In the next instant, he pressed a tumbler against her hand. "Drink."

"I swear there is a ventriloquist among us," she managed. "It's the only explanation I can come up with."

"You still haven't told me what happened."

A loud thump followed by a series of knocks had everyone stilling and holding their breaths. Everyone's eyes darted around the drawing room. If a pin had dropped, they would have heard it. Even Simmons had stopped, a tray in one hand, his right foot about to take a step.

Releasing a gush of breath that spoke of relief, Lady Audrey said, "It's the front door."

Simmons rushed out of the drawing room. Moments later, he returned and approached Lady Audrey. "It is another lost soul, my lady. Lotte Mannering. She drove her car into a ditch and has been walking for several hours."

"My heavens, she must be exhausted. Perhaps you should prepare a room for her straightaway."

"I am quite robust, my lady. The comfort of a warm fire is all I need for now."

Lotte Mannering walked in, her steps quite determined. She wore a tweed overcoat and a floppy felt hat.

"Do come in and make yourself comfortable. I am Lady Audrey and these are my guests who have found themselves in similar circumstances."

"Thank you, Lady Audrey. If you don't mind, I will keep my coat on for the time being."

"A drink, perhaps?"

"Yes, thank you."

Lotte Mannering made eye contact with the guests, nodding and smiling as she made her way to the fireplace where she stretched her hands out to capture the warmth.

Simmons handed her a drink. Turning her back to

the fire, she took a small sip and closed her eyes. When she opened them again, she smiled at Evie. "I thought I would freeze out there."

"Where were you headed?" Evie asked.

"I'm attending a house party in Slapton. At least, I think I am. Without a motor car, I'm not sure how I'll get there now."

"Slapton. Where is that?" Evie asked.

"North of Tring."

"Is your vehicle badly damaged?"

"Not at all. I had been driving at a snail's pace and just rolled into a ditch. I'll need assistance to haul it out and I know that's not going to happen until this fog lifts."

Evie found her to be quite practical. She guessed the woman might be in her early forties. Her attitude seemed to suggest she was no stranger to dealing with situations without panicking. Anyone else might have opted to remain in the car until help arrived. Lotte Mannering had decided to seek out help. Much like Tom who had employed reason, saying there had to be a house nearby and he hadn't been wrong.

"I'm regretting not taking the train." Lotte shrugged. "I've only recently acquired my motor car and have become quite attached to the idea of driving myself everywhere."

She had to be a woman of independent means, Evie thought.

"I take it you too were stranded."

Evie nodded.

"Were you on your way somewhere… I'm sorry, I should have introduced myself properly. I'm Lotte Mannering."

Evie introduced herself. "And this is Tom Winchester and Miss Cynthia Gallagher. Tom and I were headed to a nearby village." Rather than provide exact details about their trip, Evie told her about the séance.

Lotte Mannering took it all in her stride, either because death did not shock her or because the cold had really seeped into her bones.

"Truly? And the man died only last night?"

"Yes." Evie glanced around the drawing room. Locating Eleanor Barton, she pointed her out to Lotte Mannering.

"Séances are becoming rather popular these days," Lotte said. "I don't understand the need for an intermediary. If someone wishes to contact me from the great beyond, they should come straight to me."

"I quite agree." Evie nodded. "Although, I don't see the point."

"No, indeed. Everyone should try to say everything they need to while they are alive. Of course, there are exceptions. I can well imagine the urgent need to ask where the gold is hidden."

"Gold?" Evie could not have looked more puzzled.

When Lotte Mannering smiled, she realized she had been speaking about hidden treasures. "Oh, yes. Of course."

Lotte turned to Cynthia. "And what do you do, Miss Gallagher?"

Cynthia told Lotte Mannering about the article she was writing about Christmas.

"It seems an odd time of the year to be out and about. Especially in this weather. But there you have it." Lotte Mannering finished her drink and removed her coat. "None of us can stand still. Personally, I find myself constantly dashing about the place. People to see, places to be."

As the new arrival chatted with Cynthia, Evie studied her.

Lotte Mannering had said she'd been headed to Slapton. Could they believe her or had she spent the last few minutes talking with the killer?

Evie shook her head.

The police were investigating. No one could actually say anything about Mr. Barton being killed. Not until the police made it official.

Evie edged toward Tom. "Well? What do you think?"

"About what? I'm still waiting for you to tell me what happened before I came in."

"Oh, nothing... I'm referring to the intrepid traveler."

"Are you making an attempt to connect her to Mr. Barton's death?"

"She might have been trying to make her escape. We have made certain claims about being caught in this fog but we could just as easily have been lying."

"You want to hold everyone suspect, including yourself?"

She would like to do something other than attend a séance. Despite what she had told Tom, she would much rather remain in the land of the living and leave everyone... everything else to rest in peace.

Lady Audrey clapped her hands and drew everyone's attention to her. "Could you all please take a moment to decide if you wish to join us in the library. I should warn you, this might not be for the faint of heart. We want to go into this with an open mind and a belief that anything is possible. Remember, spirits have feelings too."

Tom snorted as he asked, "Are you still keen to participate? It looks to me as if you have already had a close encounter with a ghostly presence and the two of you did not quite hit it off."

Evie tipped the glass of whiskey and drank the lot. "I don't dare miss it."

A couple of the guests exchanged uncertain glances. Cynthia shrugged, and followed Evie and Tom out of the drawing room.

Simmons had set up a round table in the library

with eight chairs.

"Which would you like to be?" Evie asked. "A participant or an observer?"

"Since my job is to watch your back, I believe I will hover nearby."

Relief swept through Evie. She could not explain the presence she had felt in the drawing room. For all she knew, it might have been a draft. The curtains had been drawn, so she couldn't look out of the window to see if the wind had picked up. It didn't sound windy.

Yes, indeed. She felt comforted knowing Tom stood nearby watching her back.

Taking her place at the table, she wondered if she had any firm beliefs on the matter of the spiritual world. Evie knew she preferred to live in the here and now, but she couldn't think of a defining moment which had determined her way of living and thinking. Yes, she'd mourned her loss and had spent some time thinking about the past, but she had eventually moved on. It had never occurred to try to contact Nicholas.

Did she believe in ghosts?

Her great uncle Hadley had told the most chilling ghost stories at Christmas time. She and her cousins had sat around him holding their hands and teasing each other into running off to seek the comfort of a motherly hug.

One of their houses back home in America had an old cabin that had been built a hundred years before.

On windy nights, it sounded as if it groaned and moaned and there were stories about the man who had built it. Stories about him haunting the cabin. Since the cabin sat on the edge of the estate, she had never bothered to venture out there to seek out the truth. In fact, she had always reasoned there were stories told about their neighbor's eccentric nature, but she had never once been tempted into proving the rumors either way so why should she bother about a haunted cabin?

On the other hand, just because she hadn't seen something didn't necessarily mean it didn't exist. So, she supposed she did believe in ghosts. Up to a point.

Cynthia sat next to her. "This should be interesting."

Evie turned slightly to see who else had decided to join them. Sir Kenneth had chosen to sit on a large chair in a corner, his whiskey in his hands. Cynthia's friend, Martin Shay, chose a chair by a bookcase.

The architect, Matthew Ashby smiled down at Evie and sat down next to her.

John Arthurs sat in a corner with a book. Evie remembered he had come into the library to look at the vast collection so perhaps he wasn't aware of the fact everyone had been given a choice.

The widow, Eleanor Barton, stood by one of the chairs, her hands wrapped around the back. She looked uncertain but then Elsbeth walked up to her and murmured an encouraging word, so she sat down.

Lotte Mannering stood nearby as if trying to decide

if she should observe or step forward and participate.

Lady Audrey looked around the library. "It seems we have all decided to participate in one way or another." She drew out a chair and sat down next to Elsbeth.

The *bohemian* glanced around the table. "There are two empty chairs. Would anyone else care to join us?"

"Perhaps Mr. Arthurs?" Lady Audrey suggested.

The book buyer adjusted his glasses. "Me? I'm not sure I would be of any use."

"That's quite all right, Mr. Arthurs," Elsbeth said. "We only wish to have a full circle of people."

Evie thought the problem would be solved by simply removing a couple of chairs instead of forcing people to sit at the table.

"I'll sit at the table."

Everyone turned to see Mr. Anthony Rupert being nudged back into his chair by his wife. It seemed Mrs. Rupert did not wish her husband to be in any way associated with the proceedings.

To Evie's surprise, Mr. Rupert insisted and came to join them at the table.

Evie suspected that had been the first time Mr. Rupert had exercised his right to decide.

Lady Audrey looked up at Lotte Mannering. "Would you care to join us?"

"I'm not sure. I didn't know the deceased…"

"We prefer to call them dearly departed," Elsbeth corrected.

"Well, I didn't know him."

"That is of no consequence. We merely require a number of people to form a circle."

"Very well." Lotte took her place next to Cynthia.

Simmons finished lighting some candles and turned the lights off. The scene had been set, Evie thought.

Elsbeth directed everyone to hold hands. Thinking her hands felt slightly clammy, Evie brushed them against her skirt and then took hold of Cynthia's hand. Turning to Mr. Ashby, she smiled at him. His arms were crossed over his chest and he appeared to be having seconds thoughts.

"I suppose there's no harm in this," he finally said and took Evie's hand.

"If we are all ready," Elsbeth said. "Could you all clear your minds and think welcoming thoughts. I will now send out an invitation to Mr. Barton."

The door opened.

Everyone gasped.

"That was quick," Cynthia whispered. "Mr. Barton must be eager to speak to his wife."

A footman entered the library and searched for Simmons. He walked toward him, bumping into a table along the way. When he reached Simmons, they had a whispered conversation.

Simmons cleared his throat and walked toward Sir Kenneth. An exchange ensued after which Sir Kenneth excused himself.

"Do carry on without me," he said.

"Let us begin," Elsbeth announced. She drew in a deep breath, her eyes closed and she began to issue an invitation to Mr. Barton's ghostly presence.

"You are among friends here, Mr. Barton, and your wife is eager to speak with you. She misses you very much. If you could find a way to let us know you are here."

A candle flickered.

Evie couldn't be sure, but she thought someone stood nearby and must have moved or breathed too hard.

Someone cleared their throat. Another person shifted.

Elsbeth changed tactics, inviting a spirit guide to show Mr. Barton the way. "Guide him to us. Help us reunite him with his wife for one final farewell."

Mrs. Barton gasped.

"Did you feel him?" Elsbeth asked, her tone excited.

"I… I'm not sure. I think I did. A voice… whispered in my mind. Elie, it said. That's what my dearest used to call me. Elie."

"Did it sound near or far away?" Elsbeth asked.

"It sounded in my head."

"Talk to him, Eleanor."

Mrs. Barton cleared her throat. "Miles? Miles, is that you?"

Evie thought she felt the table wobble slightly.

Reasoning with herself, she decided she had imagined it.

Then, it happened again.

Her elbows rested on the edge of the table and no other part of her body came into contact with the solid structure.

Yes, she had definitely felt the table moving.

There had to be a reasonable explanation, she thought. Someone had made the table move.

She felt Cynthia's hand resting lightly on hers. Matthew Ashby's hand also rested lightly on hers.

Reason told her they were not responsible.

To prove it, she lifted her leg until her knee pressed against the table. It took some effort and she sensed the tension in the rest of her body. If either Cynthia or Matthew had been responsible for trying to make things more interesting by moving the table, Evie would have sensed their efforts in the pressure of their hands.

Would a spirit have the power to lift a table? If they did, then they would also have the ability to speak. Why be so dramatic?

The table could not have been moved by a ghost.

They were probably not even allowed to interact with those they'd left behind. In which case, they would take the most direct form of communication before they were ushered away by... some spiritual overseer.

Also, no one else had seemed to sense the movement. So, she must have imagined it.

Pleased with her deductive thinking, Evie stretched her legs out and crossed them at the ankles. It was all utter nonsense, she thought and gave a small nod.

"Lady Woodridge? Did you feel something?" Elsbeth asked. "Is the spirit trying to communicate through you?"

As she was about to answer, she felt a sharp stab of pain on her foot and she yelped and straightened. "Argh!"

"Has he taken possession of you? Don't fight him. Welcome him, Lady Woodridge. Embrace him and allow him to speak through you."

"Miles!" Eleanor Barton exclaimed.

"Eli… I mean, Mrs. Barton. I do apologize," Evie said.

"That's quite all right, my dearest Miles. It wasn't your fault, I'm sure."

Evie shook her head. "No, I didn't mean to…"

"I know you didn't mean to die, but you must know there is no going back. You must find peace. Everything is all right now."

Evie felt dreadful. "I'm sorry. Honestly…"

"I forgive you, Miles. Do not linger because of me."

"I mean, I'm sorry, but he's not here."

"Has he left already?" Mrs. Barton gasped and looked up. "Miles, my dearest. Farewell. Farewell."

CHAPTER 10

"Y̶ou have a strong presence, Lady Woodridge. It does not surprise me that Mr. Barton chose you to channel him. How do you feel?" the *bohemian*, Elsbeth, asked.

Evie hoped she hadn't upset Eleanor Barton. She had tried to explain but the woman had misunderstood her. It had all happened so quickly. What if this sent her over the edge?

It would be her fault.

"Distraught," Evie said.

Elsbeth nodded. "Yes, that's understandable. Especially if you have never experienced something like it before. Did you sense a light within you?"

A light? That's when Evie remembered. Someone had kicked her. She'd instinctively closed her eyes and, yes… she had seen lights bursting in her mind's eye as the pain had shot up her leg.

Her ankle would be black and blue tomorrow.

Who would do such a thing?

Had it been deliberate or an accident? Had someone stretched their legs out as she had done and accidentally kicked her?

"How are you feeling, my dear?" Lady Audrey asked the widow.

"I'm… relieved. Miles sounded well. I know Miles… or rather, I knew him. He would not have been able to rest in peace without saying a final farewell. In life, he'd always been meticulous." Eleanor Barton turned to Evie. "Thank you. Thank you from the bottom of my heart. I hope you did not suffer any great discomfort, but know that you have given a grieving widow some peace of mind." She pressed her hand to her chest and bowed her head.

Evie could not bring herself to deny the widow her peace of mind.

"Lights, please, Simmons," Lady Audrey said. "I believe we have concluded our business with the spirit world. There will be refreshments in the drawing room."

Cynthia leaned toward Evie. "How did it feel?"

"Pardon?"

"To have Mr. Barton's spirit take over your body."

"I'm not sure I have the words to describe it."

Excusing herself, Evie stood up and strode toward Tom who had remained standing by the window.

"Someone kicked me," Evie said in a hushed whisper.

Tom smiled. "Who would do such a thing just as you were being possessed by a spirit?"

"Not you too."

"Are you denying it happened?"

"Of course, I am. Mrs. Barton turned my apology into... a circus."

"You should be pleased," he said. "You offered comfort to the poor woman and helped her find closure."

Turning, she looked directly at the table. "You had an uninterrupted view of the table. Did you see anyone move?"

"You." Tom could barely suppress his laughter. "You nearly jumped out of your chair."

She tried to remember where everyone had been seated. "I think it was Lotte Mannering. She kicked me."

"I doubt her legs are long enough to have reached you."

"I'd stretched my legs out."

"When?" he asked.

Evie rolled her eyes. "Just as I was supposedly being possessed by Mr. Barton's spirit."

"Maybe that's what happens when a spirit takes possession of you."

Only one other person remained in the library. They watched John Arthurs running his fingers along a book spine and then setting it down before leaving.

"Shall we join the others?" Tom asked.

Giving a reluctant nod, she headed toward the door only to stop as it opened. She heard Tom laughing again.

"I believe the spirits are not quite done with you yet."

The door opened wider and Sir Kenneth walked in. "Ah, Lady Woodridge. I'd just been looking for you." Sir Kenneth closed the door and gestured to a group of chairs. "If I could have a moment of your time, please."

"Certainly, Sir Kenneth."

"I've just had the most curious telephone conversation," he said. "The local pub owner told me a woman had been asking questions about you earlier today. At least, that is the conclusion I reached. As in… she was asking specifically about you, not by name but rather by description. The pub owner's name is Wilkins. He said he heard several versions from different people, all of whom had been approached by a woman who seemed to fit the description of our latest arrival, Lotte Mannering. Not too tall. Robust looking with a round face."

That could have been anyone, Evie thought.

Regardless, she turned to Tom. "I knew it. She lied. If she had been in the village, her motor car could not have broken down on the way to Slapton because Slapton is many miles away from the village and to the north," Evie reasoned and turned to Sir Kenneth. "Did you say she did not ask about me by name?"

"That is correct. She merely described a woman who fit your description. A woman of status traveling with a male companion. Wilkins suggested she try our house because we are known for sheltering travelers. Of course, he hasn't met you so he couldn't say for sure you would be here. Why do you think she is looking for you? If, indeed, she is."

"I cannot possibly say, but thank you for passing on the information, Sir Kenneth."

"Do you think she might have something to do with Mr. Barton's death?" Sir Kenneth asked. "Her behavior does sound rather suspicious. Unless, of course, she mentioned looking for you when she arrived at the house."

"No, she did not say anything." Evie looked at Tom who sat opposite her brushing his finger across his chin as if in deep thought.

"Sir Kenneth, may I use your telephone, please?" Evie asked.

"Yes, of course. You'll find it in my study. The room on the right at the end of the entrance hall."

"Thank you."

Sir Kenneth nodded and stood up. "I think I will go keep an eye on Lotte Mannering."

Evie waited until Sir Kenneth had left the library to ask, "What do you have to say about that?"

"Honestly? Lotte Mannering didn't ask about you by name and when she met you, she did not mention anything about looking for you. What's there to say? She's looking for someone who fits your description. It could be a coincidence."

"How many women do you know who look like me?"

"Tall, brunette with a curious disposition to question everything and anyone?" He tried to maintain a serious face but failed.

"Laugh if you like. My life might be in danger." She didn't wait for him to comment. She stood up only to sink down again.

"What?" he asked.

Evie gasped. "After introducing herself to Lady Audrey, Lotte Mannering went directly to the fireplace where we were standing and she engaged me in conversation. Me and only me."

"And?"

"That has to mean something."

Tom walked up to a table and poured some whiskey into a glass. "Would you like one?"

"No, thank you. I need my wits about me."

Looking at the glass, he set it down again. "As you

said, if she is traveling to Slapton and her motor car drove into a ditch near Sir Kenneth's house, she would not have been anywhere near the village. Not yet, at least."

"I'm not sure I quite put it like that, but... yes."

"I think I need to run through it again... Before her motor car ended up in a ditch, she'd been headed for Slapton," Tom mused out loud as if still trying to make sense of it all. "Let's see... She drove into a ditch, decided to walk and ended up here." He gave a firm nod. "Yes, in theory, her next stop would have been the village. In reality, she's already been there. That can only mean... she doubled back or she drove into a ditch as she was headed this way from the village."

"Oh. I suppose we should have asked if her motor car is south from here or north."

"We know the answer to that," he said. "It's north because she drove here from the village."

Evie and Tom made their way to Sir Kenneth's study where Evie placed her call.

"Detective Inspector O'Neill. My apologies for tele-phoning you so late in the evening."

"Lady Woodridge. What an unexpected surprise."

"Oh, you don't sound surprised, detective." Evie heard him sigh and thought to add another apology. "I do hope I have not caught you at an inconvenient time. I would hate to impose on you."

"I'm sure you are dealing with an urgent matter, my lady."

"As a matter of fact… Yes, I am." She explained about Lotte Mannering. "I believe she is… What's the word… Tailing me."

"Tailing you?"

Evie conferred with Tom who gave a nod of agreement.

"Yes, tailing me. I wish to find out who she is and why she is following me."

"Where exactly are you, my lady?"

Evie gave him a brief explanation about being at Sir Kenneth's house.

"And you say she is staying there in the house?" the detective asked.

"Yes. I suppose you wish to know why I haven't asked her myself."

"The thought did occur…"

"I don't wish to… tip her off. As I said, we are marooned in this house."

"Marooned?"

"Oh, yes. Did I not mention that part?" She added to the brief summary she'd already given him but excluded all unnecessary details.

"Forgive me for asking, my lady, but what exactly are you doing there?"

"It's rather a long story, detective."

"I'd be surprised if it wasn't, my lady. And yet I'm still interested in hearing about it."

"It... It involves a small child's heartfelt wish which I intend to fulfill, no matter what." Evie gasped.

"That gasp sounded ominous, my lady. Whenever you gasp, you tend to have some stray thought which usually leads you to an outrageous conclusion."

"Yes, indeed. I believe my granny is behind all this."

The detective's subtle groan suggested he had just rolled his eyes.

"Toodles has arranged for someone to tail you? Why doesn't that surprise me?"

Evie smiled at his use of her granny's moniker. It seemed everyone in her inner circle had chosen to accept her granny's encouragement to use her nickname instead of a formal way of address with surprising ease. Then again, Toodles did like to get her way...

"You have been tremendously helpful, detective."

"I have? I'm not sure what I did, but you are welcome."

"Yes, indeed, a tremendous help. I could not have made the connection without you. I wonder if you might grant me another moment of your time."

"Yes, of course. I have nothing but time for you, my lady."

Evie ignored the slight hint of teasing in his tone.

"There is a gentleman by the name of John Arthurs staying in the house."

"Is he stranded there too?"

"Yes. Anyhow, he claims to be in the book buying business."

"And you'd like to verify his credentials."

Evie nodded. "If you could, please. Also… There is a gentleman by the name of Matthew Ashby. He claims to be an architect."

"Did he lose his way in the fog too?" the detective asked.

"That's what he claims."

"And you don't believe him?"

"It begins to sound odd and perhaps a little suspicious when there are so many people losing themselves in the fog… at this time of the year."

"So many people? Exactly how many?"

Evie listed them. "That's seven people. Then there's Elsbeth, the *bohemian*. She too is staying the night. Although, strictly speaking, she is not stranded. She's here by choice. Then there's Mrs. Barton."

"My apologies for interrupting you, my lady. Did you say, *bohemian*?"

"Yes. She's the one who performed the séance."

"A séance?" the detective's voice hitched.

"Yes. She wanted to contact Mrs. Barton's husband."

"And did she?"

"More or less… They all believe he spoke through me. Anyhow, we're getting off topic here…"

"Oh, are we?"

"Again, my apologies for imposing on your time, detective. But as you can see, there is a house full of suspects."

After a moment of silence, the detective said, "I take it you have cleared Lotte Mannering because you now believe your grandmother is responsible for… hiring her?"

"Yes."

"And you now suspect the other guests of… Ah, yes. This is where I become a little confused. Perhaps I missed that vital piece of information. Are you afraid they too are, as you say, tailing you?"

"Oh, no. I think one of them is a killer." Evie pressed the telephone to her ear and listened to the silence. "Detective?"

The silence lengthened and then he said, "You mentioned the possibility of there being a killer. I assume there is also a victim."

"Yes, yes, indeed. Mr. Barton. Although, it is not official yet."

"So, the local police are investigating…"

"I believe so. They haven't spoken with us yet. From what I understand, they will be carrying out interviews tomorrow." She went on to provide more information about Miles Barton's death.

"And his widow was present at the séance, the one where you channeled her husband..."

"Yes. I believe we are on the same page now."

Tom came to stand closer to Evie and said, "Detective, it's Tom Winchester. In answer to the question you have been eager to ask, no, we have not been drinking. Well… perhaps a glass or two, but nothing to cause a state of inebriation."

"Thank you for clarifying that, Mr. Winchester."

Evie turned to Tom. "He says thank you."

The detective cleared his throat. "I think I should extend my colleagues the courtesy of a telephone call. Where might I reach you, my lady?"

Evie looked around Sir Kenneth's desk. Finding the telephone number, she gave it to him. Thanking him, she wished him a good night and disconnected the call.

Turning, she found herself alone in the study. Before she could wonder where Tom had disappeared to, he returned.

Holding up a newspaper, he said, "The woman who is parading around as Lotte Mannering is actually Mrs. May Harcourt, lady detective."

Evie stared at the grainy photograph. "My goodness. How did I not see it before? Well done, Tom. Do you think we're on the right track and Lotte Mannering is the woman who asked about my whereabouts in the village?"

"I think it would be safe to assume that, yes."

"And what do you think about Toodles being behind it all?"

Tom laughed. "Oh, yes. I wouldn't be surprised if she is. It's just the sort of thing she would do. Although, since I'm traveling with you, I fail to see why she would take the extra precaution of safeguarding her heiress granddaughter."

Evie gave a firm nod. "I think we should confront Lotte Mannering. But not tonight. Honestly, I cannot face anyone tonight. Not after the séance."

"Where is your sense of adventure?"

Evie paced around the study. "Toodles has to be responsible for setting that woman on my trail. She must be. Otherwise, my life might really be in danger."

Shrugging, Tom said, "I suppose we'll have to wait until we return to ask her why she took such measures."

"Not necessarily. I think she meant to test me. She is determined to steer me toward a career as a lady detective. I believe… Yes, I do believe she meant to test me."

"In that case, you have managed to prove yourself. Countess, you have unmasked a seasoned detective. Don't you want to crow?"

"Oh, I suppose I do. Fine, let's go and join the others."

CHAPTER 11

"You've already had a lengthy chat with Matthew Ashby. Would you care to dig a little deeper?" Evie asked before they entered the drawing room.

"I thought you were only going to question Lotte Mannering," Tom said.

"You heard me telling the detective we have a house full of suspects. There is still the matter of Miles Barton."

Tom did not comment except to say, "What do you wish to find out about Matthew Ashby?"

"He claims to be on his way to a family gathering. Find out if there's another reason for him to be in the area."

"I see. So, we're to reject all explanations given by

the guests and suspect them of being here for entirely different reasons."

Evie gave it some thought and then nodded. "Yes. It's a roundabout way of saying guilty until proven innocent. We never think to doubt what people say. How does one know they are telling the truth? It's when something such as an unexpected death happens that we need to begin to question and doubt."

"That did not come from a Sigmund Freud book. Have you moved on to someone new?"

"I might have. Remember a while back Detective O'Neill mentioned a detective working... I think he said Germany or was it Austria? Anyhow, there are papers written on the subject of criminology and I thought it would tie in well with my Freud books."

"While I speak with Mr. Ashby, what will you do?" Tom asked.

Evie considered her options. "I will tackle Lotte Mannering directly by ignoring her. If she seeks me out, then I'll know she is the one who asked about me in the village."

They walked into the drawing room and found everyone engaged in murmured conversations. Everyone including Mr. and Mrs. Rupert. Mr. Anthony Rupert appeared to be quite animated. Perhaps his moment away from his wife's influence had given him a taste of the freedom he might otherwise enjoy if she did not insist on keeping him by her side.

Not for the first time, Evie wished the police had talked to them today instead of leaving it until the next day. They were either not taking the matter seriously, or they had found a solid lead to pursue, one which had led them away from the group of travelers.

She saw Lotte Mannering seated alone near the fireplace, her gaze fixed on the flames. Could she assume Lotte found no reason to engage the others in conversation because she only had one sole purpose in mind?

She had her answer when Lotte glanced away from the flames and saw Evie. She straightened and smiled at Evie.

Instead of responding by walking toward her, Evie searched for Cynthia and found her by the window talking with her traveling companion, Martin Shay.

Smiling up at Evie, she said, "I've been trying to find out if anyone saw anything curious in the library. Martin says he thought he saw the table moving. I think I might have felt it move. But I'm not sure."

"It would have been easy enough for someone to apply pressure with their legs," Evie said.

"Well, I know it wasn't me."

Had Lotte moved it right before she kicked Evie?

Why? To create a distraction? Or perhaps to bring the séance to an end.

"I trust Martin. He has a keen eye for detail."

Cynthia studied Evie. "I suppose you didn't really channel the spirit of Mr. Barton."

Evie gave her a small, apologetic smile. "You look disappointed."

Cynthia shrugged. "It would be nice to have proof of the afterlife. It's strange. When Mrs. Barton first arrived, I thought she might have been scared of the possibility her husband could be contacted. Almost as if she didn't want someone talking with him."

Yes, and she hadn't actually asked any pertinent questions about his death. Evie tried to recall what had happened. How had the séance ended? Indeed, how had it all started?

After a moment, she remembered Mrs. Barton claiming to have heard her name spoken... in her head.

A timely distraction, Evie couldn't help thinking. From what? The possibility the *bohemian* might actually contact her husband's spirit?

She happened to glance away and caught sight of Tom signaling to her. Excusing herself, Evie joined Tom in a corner.

"Have you made a significant discovery?" she asked.

"Perhaps I have. It seems there is a shortage of land for sale. Or rather, too many architectural firms competing for the few parcels of land available. Mr. Ashby is under pressure to assist in procuring land."

"That's interesting. Do you think he would kill someone in order to secure a sale?"

They both stared at each other for a moment.

Then, Evie gasped.

"Heavens, there's that gasp of yours. Did you just have a bright idea?" Tom asked.

"I think so. Or, rather, clarification. Remember, we questioned Mr. Ashby's story. He claims to be on his way to visit relatives, yet he also said he nearly collided with Cynthia and Martin Shay."

"So, you're suggesting he might have been to see Mr. Barton?"

Evie nodded. "We would need to find out if Mr. Barton owned any land."

Tom glanced away for a moment. "I think Sir Kenneth might be able to assist us in that matter."

Evie played around with a gruesome scenario. Wincing, she pictured Mr. Ashby, desperate to hold on to his job through any means, including killing the owner of some valuable land because he refused to sell.

Turning, she looked to the widow. Would she agree to dispose of some land in order to secure her lifestyle? That led Evie to wonder how Mr. Barton had funded his travels…

She saw a footman enter the drawing room. He walked directly toward Simmons and delivered a message. Someone had arrived, Evie thought.

At this late hour?

Sir Kenneth left the drawing room. It had to be the

police. What else would compel the host of an impromptu house party into abandoning his guests?

Lady Audrey noticed her husband's exit and visibly fretted, both hands pressed to her chest.

Did she sense something in the air? If she did, Lady Audrey did a splendid job of hiding it as she turned and smiled at her guests who had all noticed their hosts' departure.

"More tea or coffee? Or perhaps a song."

Everyone looked aghast at the idea of singing at a time when they were held enthralled by what they must have sensed as an intriguing development in the making.

Sir Kenneth returned. Clearing his throat, he announced, "Detective Inspector Warren and his colleague, Detective Inspector Clarke will be joining us tonight. The weather conditions have worsened and... they sought refuge here."

A likely story, Evie thought.

Both men wore the same suits they'd had on earlier that day. Had they narrowed their search?

Simmons stood in the background, his posture erect, and his expression severe as he glanced around the room. If he held any opinions about the new guests, he did not betray them.

The widow, Mrs. Eleanor Barton, sat next to Mr. and Mrs. Rupert, a handkerchief in her hands, her eyes slightly widened. Was she intrigued or concerned?

Tom walked toward Evie. He carried two cups and displayed a teasing smile.

"Is that coffee?" Evie asked.

"Yes, I thought you might need some. I believe this is about to turn into a long night."

"Do you believe the story about the detectives being stranded?"

Tom lifted the cup to his lips. "Not for a moment."

Evie tasted her coffee. "Thank you for remembering the sugar."

Tom walked around her and went to stand on her right.

"Was that a strategic move?" she asked.

"Yes. I noticed Lotte Mannering about to come this way and thought to give her the idea we are holding a private conversation."

"She is definitely keen to talk to me. I'd like to see how far she'll go."

"You want to force her to make a mistake?"

Evie glanced up at him. "Does that make me wicked?" She made a discreet gesture toward the detectives. "They must have come to their senses and realized their mistake in not talking to the people here."

"Or worse," Tom said. "They have reason to believe the killer is among us and are here to make sure they don't strike again."

"They don't seem to be terribly interested in talking

with us. Do you think they are trying to make us nervous?"

"And force the killer into making a mistake the way you are forcing Lotte Mannering? I think Toodles might be onto something. You should really give this business of detecting serious thought."

Evie raised an eyebrow. "I hope you are not suggesting I am bored with my comfortable life and need a distraction."

"I'm merely pointing out your talents, which might be going to waste."

Evie gave him a bright smile. "How kind of you to say so." As she looked down at her coffee cup, she saw Mr. Hector Hollings watching her. "What do we know about him?"

"Who?"

"Hector Hollings."

"I remember him saying he visits a lot of libraries. I have no idea what he does or where he comes from or what brought him here. Only that his motor car ran out of gas and he arrived here this morning." He took a sip of his coffee and without looking at Evie, added, "You want me to find out all I can."

"What a wonderful idea. If we're smart, we might be able to deduce something significant before the detectives do and then we'll… Heavens, then we'll prove Toodles right. I should do something of note with my life."

"Is that what she has been expecting of you?" Tom asked.

"Honestly, I'm surprised she hasn't encouragement me to go on the stage. You know she wanted to be an actress…"

"And you think she wishes to live vicariously through her grandchildren?"

"Actually, I think she thinks we have too many advantages without having earned them. It's this new age of women breaking free of their typical roles. Toodles has nothing but admiration for them…"

A footman made his way toward Evie. "My lady. There is an Inspector O'Neill on the telephone for you."

The footman took her cup and she hurried to take the call. Sounding slightly out of breath, she said, "Inspector. I believe it is my turn to sound surprised."

"My lady. I didn't think I'd be able to provide you with any valuable information… As it happens, I have some houseguests staying for Christmas. One of them has an interest in horticulture and belongs to several societies. I mentioned the conversation we'd had and he recognized Mr. Barton's name. The society had been funding Mr. Barton's expeditions…"

Evie guessed the rest and thought the funds had most likely dried up.

"However, he had recently met with some competition and the available funds have gone to someone else."

As the detective continued, she tried to think how someone with a keen interest in a subject would go about raising funds for his expeditions.

"Anyhow, I thought you might want to know. In the past, you have managed to turn otherwise insignificant information into vital clues."

"How kind of you to say so, detective. What you've told me provides a new insight." She had no idea what sort of insight, but it all had to mean something. She did not believe the police had found themselves stranded by accident. Something had brought them here. "Thank you, detective. Oh, and by the way, your colleagues have decided to become stranded too."

Walking back to the drawing room, Evie turned her thoughts to Lotte Mannering. "Perhaps the woman could be of some use," she whispered. First, she would need to find out why Lotte had been asking about her. Or rather, she would need Lotte to confirm Toodles' involvement.

Looking up, Evie decided now would be a good time to start.

Lotte Mannering stood outside the drawing room. Had she followed Evie? Had she pressed her ear to the door and overheard her conversation with the detective?

Inspired, Evie asked, "Are you trying to avoid the police? Is that why you came out here?"

Lotte could not have looked more surprised.

"Your absence will only end up drawing attention to yourself," Evie continued.

"I'm not sure I know what you are talking about, my lady."

"Perhaps we could start with your real name."

"Pardon?"

"Would you like me to help you?"

Lotte Mannering lifted her chin.

"Let me see… You don't really look like a Lotte to me. Mary? No… Not Mary. May. Yes, that rather suits you. Mrs. May Harcourt, lady detective."

CHAPTER 12

*M*ay Harcourt's entire demeanor changed in the blink of an eye. Evie only now noticed the difference. Before, she had looked rather nondescript. In fact, she had looked like an ordinary person, albeit a well-to-do one, from any village in the county.

Now, she had acquired a no-nonsense appearance. She stood taller and her face had hardened.

"We saw a photograph of you in the newspaper," Evie said. "Admittedly, we did not make the connection straightaway. Now that I look at you closely, I see you have a firmly set mouth. Your hair is different in the photograph, but that's something that can be easily changed. Tell me, do you often disguise yourself?"

Lotte Mannering huffed. "I am truly speechless and you have no idea what it took for me to admit that."

Evie gave a casual shrug. "Tom and I tend to be suspicious of everyone. I'm sure you have no trouble duping the average criminal." Her eyebrows lifted. "Are you under the impression I am some sort of criminal?"

The edge of Lotte Mannering's lip lifted. "I was led to believe you had been involved in several thefts."

"Truly?"

"I was told you talk your way into grand houses to study the layout and then send in your accomplices."

"I hope you realize that is an entirely fabricated account of my activities."

This seemed to surprise the lady detective. "And how would you describe your activities?"

"Some would say I am a busybody," Evie declared. "I can, however, assure you I have never participated in any nefarious activities. I'm sorry to say… You have been misled by my mischievous grandmother."

"Toodles?"

Evie rolled her eyes. "Thank you for confirming her involvement. I have no idea what she might have been thinking."

"She is your grandmother?"

"Yes, indeed, she is."

"Is this some sort of prank?"

"I'm inclined to say yes, it is. However, my granny works in mysterious ways." Evie clasped her hands together. "Do you wish to continue denying your real identity?" When the lady detective didn't answer, Evie smiled. "In that case, you might be of some assistance."

"I'm listening."

"Well, Lotte… Oh, may I continue to call you Lotte? It would simplify matters."

The detective nodded. "Yes, I should hate to have to explain myself to Sir Kenneth. He has been… a jovial host. What's on your mind, my lady?"

A couple of minutes after Lotte Mannering walked back in to the drawing room, Evie followed. She headed straight for Tom. "I have recruited a third person," she whispered and told him about her encounter with the lady detective.

"She is now working for you?"

"Yes." Evie noticed the detectives had split up and where chatting with the other guests. "Do you have any interesting observations to report?"

"You sound so officious." Tom smiled. "I've been standing here long enough to have noticed several furtive glances between Mr. Ashby and Mrs. Barton."

"The architect and the widow?"

"Yes. It might have been going on for a while now."

And he had only now noticed the exchanges because she had asked him to delve into Matthew Ashby's activities.

"It's a pity we can't drive into the village just yet," Evie said. "I would love to talk with the locals. Someone must have seen something or seen someone hovering around the village."

"I am willing to bet everyone in this room has been to the village," Tom said.

"And I would be inclined to agree with you. Meaning, they all lied about their destinations when they were caught in the fog."

As someone walked by them, Tom lowered his voice, "I'm sure the police have already talked to everyone in the village. It must have been at the top of their list."

"I'm not so sure," Evie mused. "In fact, I think they might have passed a verdict of death by misadventure from the start."

"Actually, they find the incident quite puzzling."

She turned to him, surprised. "Have you spoken with the detectives?"

"Certainly. They are extremely puzzled. No signs of a break-in. No footprints around the house. No murder weapon."

Evie asked, "Did they at least question the staff?"

"Yes. All loyal to Mr. Barton. In fact, as Sir Kenneth said, they don't have a bad word to say about him. And, before you ask," Tom said, "the answer is yes. Mr. and Mrs. Barton's house sits on a large park. As Mr. Barton had no interest other than his books and plants, the park remains largely ignored."

"Didn't he have people working for him?"

"It took some doing, but Mrs. Barton eventually said his journeys abroad were taking their toll on their finances. They had to let a couple of people go."

"I see. I suppose this is as good a time as any to tell you about my conversation with the detective."

"Which one?" Tom asked.

"O'Neill."

"What did he say?"

"It ties in with what you told me about the Bartons letting go of staff. Mr. Barton needed money for his expeditions. You see, he'd lost his funding."

"How on earth did the detective come up with that information so late in the evening?" Tom asked.

"One of his guests has an interest in horticulture and he recognized Mr. Barton's name."

"That was a lucky chance."

Evie mused, "I suppose in any gathering there is bound to be someone knowledgeable about something or other."

"So, what now?"

Evie stifled a yawn. "More than anything, I would like to retire for the evening. I wonder if Elsbeth would be willing to have a chat with the ghosts in my bedroom. I need all the rest I can get before our trip to the village tomorrow."

"I'm sure if you ask nicely enough she will accommodate you."

"Oh…"

"Oh?"

"I just witnessed an exchange of interesting looks, which, in my opinion, are open to interpretation."

Tom followed the direction of her glance. "Between Mrs. Barton and Mr. Matthew Ashby?"

"No, between Mrs. Barton and John Arthurs."

"The book buyer."

"Yes. She nodded and… he nodded."

"Perhaps they were acknowledging each other. I've often found myself looking around a room and suddenly clashing with someone's glance and then an awkward moment follows because we probably both think the other means to say something and we both nod for no apparent reason."

"Really? I've never noticed that oddity about you," Evie said. "I thought I was the only one who experienced silly moments."

Tom cleared his throat. "I prefer to think of them as awkward. Silliness doesn't sit well with me."

"Not manly enough?"

He refrained from commenting.

Evie tugged his sleeve. "Did you see that? Mr. Arthurs nudged his head toward the door."

The book buyer set his drink down and slipped out of the drawing room. Seconds later, Mrs. Barton yawned. Standing up, she crossed the room and had a murmured conversation with Lady Audrey. Then, she left.

"They must be meeting somewhere," Evie whispered.

"Are you about to suggest we follow them?" he asked.

"We? Oh, no. That would look too obvious. Well, go on... If you don't hurry, you'll lose them."

Tom sighed. "No need. Your new accomplice has gone after them."

"Lotte?"

"I thought her real name is May."

"It is, but I'm already accustomed to calling her Lotte. Do you think Mr. Arthurs is trying to get a foot in the door? Mr. Barton must have quite a collection of books."

"Really, Countess. I'm disappointed in you. Surely, you can come up with a better theory. They are plotting together and are, in fact, responsible for Mr. Barton's demise."

"My apologies. My mind strayed to the real reason for our journey here. We must set off early tomorrow. Mrs. Barton said there might be some things in the attic no one has claimed. I cannot return to Halton House empty-handed."

"In that case, our departure time will depend on

Mrs. Barton. However, she might be in handcuffs before then."

Lotte Mannering returned to the drawing room and walked with purpose toward them. "They went to the library. Luckily, they left the door ajar and I was able to peer inside. Mr. Arthurs is showing the widow a book. It seems he is after a similar copy and she might have it in Mr. Barton's library."

"Nothing but an innocent rendezvous," Evie declared.

"It seems we are not the only ones to notice them leaving." Tom nodded toward the door and they watched one of the detectives leaving.

Evie laughed under her breath.

"Care to share the joke?" Tom asked.

"Oh, under the circumstances, it is too silly. However… Wouldn't it be amusing if we all leave at intervals and head off in different directions. We would have the detectives going around in circles."

The detective who'd stayed behind finished his conversation with Cynthia and moved toward Evie and Tom.

"He's coming this way," Lotte said.

"Are you, by any chance, in trouble with the law?" Evie asked her.

"Not exactly, but I'm not a favorite. I have stumbled across a couple of murder scenes. They don't take kindly to outside interference."

Laughing under his breath, Tom said, "Lady Woodridge is all too familiar with police disapproval."

The detective introduced himself and proceeded to question them, starting with Lotte Mannering.

"It is our understanding you were headed toward the village when you lost control of your motor car."

Lotte lifted her chin. "I'm sure you were told a different version."

"Yes, as a matter of fact, you were seen in the village," the detective admitted.

"Lotte Mannering was looking for me," Evie piped in. "And... she found me. It's a long story and has nothing to do with your case."

The detective studied Evie. "We received a strange telephone call about you."

Evie wondered if Tom would come to her rescue as she had done for Lotte.

"It seems you have a history of being in the wrong place, my lady."

"I'm sure you'd be the first to admit crime does not discriminate. A few incidents have... orbited around me."

Instead of helping her out, Tom crossed his arms and tilted his head in amusement. A new trait he had picked up only recently, she thought. She would almost be inclined to say she had become a source of amusement for him.

"In any case, we have been nowhere near the village," Evie continued. "Not yet."

"What do you mean?" the detective asked.

Evie decided to tell him about her search for the Christmas ornaments, sparing him no detail. She even included the story about finding everyone in the stables the morning Tom had given Seth his pony.

The detective shook his head. For a moment, Evie thought he would issue her a warning to take the matter seriously, but then he smiled.

"I doubt you'll be able to improve on a pony. Every little boy wants one."

"That seems to be the general consensus, but the ornaments hold sentimental value," Evie said. "I'm sure he'll love them as much as he loves the pony."

Smiling, the detective said, "Detective Inspector O'Neill also remarked on your ability to stray off topic."

"In my defense, one has to excel at something."

CHAPTER 13

"I'm not sure the detectives will appreciate our early departure," Tom said the next morning.

"Why should it matter if we leave early in the morning? It's not as if we are guilty of killing Mr. Barton. Besides, Detective O'Neill has already vouched for us... in his own unique way."

Evie rearranged her woolen scarf. She had a thick blanket on her knees but the cold had already made its way through to her bones. Any minute now, her teeth would start chattering.

"I must say, I'm surprised Mrs. Barton drives herself. She did not strike me as an independent sort."

"What happens after you find the ornaments?" Tom asked.

"Thank you for your optimism. I do hope they have

been forgotten in a dark corner of the house. As to what we'll do... If the road conditions don't improve, we might have to consider traveling back by train."

"Yes, that is an option, but I was referring to the case."

"Oh, the one I'm supposed to avoid becoming involved in because it really is none of my business?" Evie thought about the wet handkerchief she had tucked inside her handbag. She intended taking full advantage of their visit to Mr. Barton's house.

In her opinion, the detectives had been too quick to dismiss the case or, rather, too slow to take it seriously. They were bound to have missed something.

"Is Mr. Arthurs staying close behind us?" she asked.

Tom checked the rearview mirror. "He's leaning so far forward over the steering wheel, I can see his face."

The journey was bumpy, slow and cold.

They didn't see anyone out and about in the village but everyone's chimneys were already puffing out white smoke.

When they reached the edge of the village, they saw Mrs. Barton's motor car turn into a driveway. Following her, they drove past a tall hedge and turned into the drive. A modest manor house sat at the end of the long drive. Beyond it, they could see a large park that turned into a wilderness adjoining the fields beyond.

As soon as Tom brought the motor car to a stop,

Evie jumped out and made a dash for the front door, stomping her feet to get the circulation going before entering.

"Stevens," Mrs. Barton said. "This is the Countess of Woodridge." Removing her hat and gloves, she told him about the Christmas ornaments that might have been left behind by the previous owner and sent him up to the attics to look for them. "We'll know soon enough if they are here," she said and showed Evie through to a drawing room.

Evie hoped she would have the opportunity to look around the house. Specifically, she wished to see the study where Mr. Barton had been killed, but she thought it might be tricky to get Mrs. Barton to show her the room without sounding ghoulish.

Tom caught up with her and she saw him taking in every detail of the drawing room, something he didn't normally do.

"I'll ring for some tea," Mrs. Barton said as she handed her coat to a maid. "If you'll excuse me a moment, I need to change out of these clothes."

"Yes, of course, do take your time," Evie encouraged.

As soon as Mrs. Barton closed the door behind her, Evie headed for an adjacent door. "I wonder where this leads to."

Tom chortled. "So, this is what happens when strangers are left alone in a room. They start poking around."

"It's a dining room. I suppose the study is on the opposite side of the hallway. I'm sure I can get away with wandering around the place. I suppose if someone questions me, I can pretend I have lost my voice."

They heard someone clearing their throat and both turned toward the door leading to the front entrance.

"That must be Mr. Arthurs. I'll use that as an excuse to slip out." Evie walked with determination and found the book buyer studying a portrait. "I believe the staff are otherwise engaged, Mr. Arthurs." She signaled to the drawing room. "Tom is in there. Mrs. Barton will be down momentarily."

She walked on as if she had been charged with a serious task and went through the first door to the right of the entrance.

"This," she whispered, "looks like the study." She closed the door behind her and sent her gaze skating around the room.

A large desk sat in the middle of the room with a fireplace to the side and bookcases lining one side of the room and drawings of plants covering another wall and the spaces at either side of the fireplace.

She didn't see any signs of where the attack might have occurred. Nothing had been disturbed and if it had been, someone had put everything back in its place.

The room looked spotlessly clean. Evie sniffed the air and thought she picked up a scent of vinegar. If a death took place at her house, she supposed she would want to clean it straightaway.

Mr. Barton had died the previous night.

Evie frowned.

Forgetting about the state of the room, she thought about Mrs. Barton. For a recent widow, she looked quite calm. In fact, apart from her initial state of uneasiness when she'd first appeared at the Audrey house, Mrs. Barton had been looking quite settled and even content.

She went to stand in front of the desk and looked for a possible weapon.

Mr. Barton had suffered a blow to the back of the head. Had he been sitting at his desk? Or maybe standing in front of the fireplace.

If he'd been hit from behind, then the killer had caught him by surprise and...

She turned and looked at the door directly opposite the fireplace.

"The killer entered and..." Had the killer spoken to Mr. Barton? No, because Mr. Barton would then have turned.

Walking to the door, one of the floorboards creaked. If it had made a noise when she'd entered, she hadn't noticed it.

She turned back toward the fireplace. Seeing the fire poker, she dug inside her handbag and retrieved the wet handkerchief.

A while back, she had learned the trick from Detective Inspector O'Neill. Even if the killer had used the fire poker as a weapon and then cleaned it, there might still be traces of blood.

Evie dabbed the end of the fire poker. When the handkerchief came away clean, she applied more pressure. Again, nothing.

According to the police, there had been no signs of a break-in.

Evie walked to the windows and checked the locks. They were intact. No one had forced their way into the study.

Fretting at the lack of some sort of evidence, she wiped her fingers with the handkerchief.

Looking down, Evie gasped.

The handkerchief had a faint red stain.

She swung toward the window again. Taking a closer look at the latch, she wiped it.

"Blood."

Why would there be blood on the latch? "The killer closed the window?" Surely, it would have been too cold for the window to be open. Then again, she remembered her husband used to enjoy standing at the window and breathing the night air, even in winter time. When he'd worked late into the night, he would open the window slightly saying the slight chill kept him awake and alert.

Evie stepped back enough to take in the whole

room. She pictured a scenario. The killer struck their blow. They might have taken a closer look to make sure the blow had done its job or they might have smudged their fingers on the murder weapon.

Then they noticed the window. They walked toward it and looked outside. They probably realized they would have to do something about footprints since there weren't any. Instead, they decided to close the window and that's when they left a smudge of blood on the latch...

"But what about the murder weapon? What did they use?"

She looked at the clock on the mantle. Too big, she thought. The candlestick was a possibility. Hurrying toward it, she used a clean corner of her still wet handkerchief to wipe it. Nothing.

She remembered someone had mentioned the victim had possibly fallen and hit their head against the edge of the desk.

Miles Barton had used a small stepladder to reach the top shelves of his bookcases.

Some were freestanding, while the ones directly behind the desk were built into the wall.

"Secret entrance?" Evie murmured.

Knowing she was running out of time, she pressed one of the bookcases. It did not budge. The next one she tried moved slightly.

Evie gasped.

She stood in front of the bookcase, her eyes wide. When she heard a loud knock at the front door, she nearly jumped out of her skin.

Hurried footsteps moved toward the entrance. A murmured exchange was followed by several footsteps.

The study door opened.

A man stood at the door. He was then joined by another man.

"Lady Woodridge."

Evie swallowed and then gave a stiff nod. "Detectives."

They exchanged a look that spoke of amusement.

Heavens. Had everyone made her the source of their amusement?

"Might we ask what you are doing in Mr. Barton's study?"

"Satisfying my ghoulish curiosity, of course."

"Of course. And, in the course of satisfying your ghoulish curiosity, did you happen to find something?"

Evie shrugged. "I might have."

They both sighed.

"Would you care to share your findings?" the detective asked.

They were not smiling now. Evie took that as a good sign.

At the sound of someone approaching, they all turned toward the door.

"Ah, here's Lady Woodridge," Mrs. Barton said.

Tom stood behind her and they both entered the study.

The detectives greeted her and one of them explained, "We need to have another look in your husband's study."

Mrs. Barton pressed her hand to her chest. "Yes, of course."

Detective Warren looked at Evie. "You were about to say something."

Instead of telling him outright about her findings, she fanned herself. "Is it getting hot in here? I suddenly find myself gasping for breath and feeling... quite faint."

Detective Clarke walked over to the window and unlatched it.

"I hope that window latch wasn't dusty, detective."

He looked at his fingers and then frowned.

"You might want to clean your fingers with a handkerchief."

He did as she suggested and showed the results to the other detective.

"What is it?" Mrs. Barton asked.

Tom looked at Evie and lifted an eyebrow as if questioning her tactics.

"Mrs. Barton, would you care to wait in the drawing room? My colleague and I need to focus on our investigation."

Just then, Mrs. Barton caught sight of the handkerchief. She gasped and swayed.

Catching her, Tom led her out of the study.

"Blood but no weapon," Detective Warren murmured.

"There's something else," Evie said and gestured to the bookcase behind her. "I believe it opens to another room." She pressed her back against it. When it suddenly opened, Evie lost her footing and fell back.

As she tried to regain her balance, she fell on her bottom and the bookcase closed. But not before she heard the detectives chuckling.

"Good heavens," a voice said behind her.

Evie turned and saw Mr. Arthurs holding a book.

Clearly, she had landed in the library.

"Where did you come from?" he asked.

Evie pointed toward the bookcase. "It's a secret passage leading to the study."

"How ingenious."

He helped her up. Instead of trying the bookcase again, she thought she would use the proper door. Easing it open, she saw Tom coming out of the drawing and crossing the hallway…

With Mrs. Barton standing behind him and holding a revolver.

"Oh…" Evie jumped back and eased the door shut. Turning, she pressed her finger to her lip.

Mrs. Barton.

Mrs. Barton.

She knew the police were onto her. Did she mean to kill everyone?

Evie eased the door open a notch, enough to see Mrs. Barton standing on the threshold to the study, still pointing a revolver.

Evie knew she only had seconds to act. If she didn't, Mrs. Barton would realize she was no longer in the study.

"What is happening?" Mr. Arthurs whispered, a book clutched against his chest.

Clearly, he would be of no use.

Becoming quite frantic, she searched the library.

Mr. Arthurs must have read her mind. He joined her search and surprised Evie by handing her a cricket bat.

"Oh. Thank you," she mouthed.

Scooping in a breath, she eased the door open. The moment she stepped out of the library, Mrs. Barton turned and saw her.

Evie panicked.

She was too far away to use the cricket bat. Instead, she swung it over her shoulder and flung it at Mrs. Barton at the precise moment one of the detectives took advantage of the opportunity and tackled Mrs. Barton to the floor.

"Yikes," he screamed at the bat his head.

Pandemonium broke out as Mrs. Barton screamed and struggled. The revolver went off and everyone stilled.

"Good heavens," the butler, who had been coming down the stairs, said. "You've shot Mr. Barton."

EPILOGUE

"**G**ood heavens, you've shot Mr. Barton." Tom tipped his head back and laughed at his own perfect impersonation of Stevens, the butler.

Remembering the scene, Evie laughed right along with him. "For a moment there, I thought the detective had been shot." Then, it had become clear. The bullet had put a hole in a painting of Mr. Barton.

Mrs. Barton had killed her husband all over again.

"To think you saved the day with the one object the police had been looking for. The murder weapon."

"Yes, I guess they omitted to look in the library. I actually have Mr. Arthurs to thank for that. I could not have found something to use as a weapon to save my life. In that moment of panic, I couldn't see anything. I think I must have been blind with fear."

"You were splendid, Countess."

Tom changed gears and tackled the sloping incline. They had chosen to drive the long way around to avoid becoming stranded in the fog again.

Once the road leveled and straightened, Evie said, "I can't imagine why Eleanor Barton married Miles. It could not have been for love, otherwise, she would not have killed him." She gave it some thought and then added, "She must have wanted a comfortable living. Pity he wanted to sell off part of the estate to fund his expeditions. I believe he would have sold everything off to fund his passion."

"She should have divorced him and found herself another husband," Tom said.

"I agree." Shaking her head, she mused, "I will never understand why someone would willingly risk the gallows for financial gain."

After a moment of silence, Evie beamed up at Tom. "Imagine Toodles' surprise when I return with my price."

"Are you referring to the Christmas ornaments or to Lotte Mannering?"

"The ornaments, of course. How lucky for us that Stevens found them in a corner of the attic." Evie gazed out at the landscape in all its wintry splendor. "Fine... Yes, she will be speechless when we walk in with Lotte. I suppose I should start calling her May."

"Do you really think it's wise to flaunt your victory? Toodles might take it as a challenge."

"I'm hoping it will put an end to the silly notion of me becoming a lady detective."

"I fail to see your reasoning."

"That's because I'm not really making sense." Evie yawned. "I'm exhausted." In reality, she didn't wish to talk about the reasons for bringing Lotte Mannering... or rather, May Harcourt, back to Halton House.

Evie had asked if she planned on taking a break for the holidays and May had confessed she wouldn't. Prodding, Evie had discovered May Harcourt didn't have any family. Without thinking about it, she had invited the lady detective to join them at Halton House.

"I've just had a bright idea. Instead of playing a game of charades for Christmas, we could play a sleuthing game."

"Haven't you had enough?"

"Oh, but think of the fun we'd have. Caro could join in and dress up as one of my distant relatives. You know how much she likes to do that."

Tom grumbled under his breath. "With your ability to attract mayhem into your life, I wouldn't be surprised if we end up with a real corpse..."

Smiling, Evie patted the precious box they had traveled all that way to find. "Oh, I do hope Seth likes his gift."

*****

Printed in Great Britain
by Amazon

58229663R00099